seeing cinderella

BY JENNY LUNDQUIST

ALADDIN

NEW YORK LONDON TORONTO SYDNEY NEW DELHI

WITHDRAWN

ALADDIN

Simon & Schuster Children's Publishing Division
1230 Avenue of the Americas, New York, NY 10020
First Aladdin hardcover edition March 2012
Copyright © 2012 by Jenny Lundquist
All rights reserved, including the right of reproduction
in whole or in part in any form.
ALADDIN is a trademark of Simon & Schuster, Inc., and related logo
is a registered trademark of Simon & Schuster, Inc.
For information about special discounts for bulk purchases,
please contact Simon & Schuster Special Sales at 1-866-506-1949
or business@simonandschuster.com.
The Simon & Schuster Speakers Bureau can bring authors to your live event.
For more information or to book an event contact the Simon & Schuster Speakers
Bureau at 1-866-248-3049 or visit our website at www.simonspeakers.com.
Designed by Jessica Handelman
The text of this book was set in Mrs Eaves Roman
Manufactured in the United States of America 0212 FFG
2 4 6 8 10 9 7 5 3 1
Library of Congress Control Number 2011922407
ISBN 978-1-4424-4550-5 (hc)
ISBN 978-1-4424-2926-0 (pbk)
ISBN 978-1-4424-2927-7 (eBook)

To Ryan, who sees me

Acknowledgments

This book wouldn't exist without the love and support of so many others. A big thanks to my rockstar of an agent, Kerry Sparks, for believing in me and picking me out of the slush.

Tremendous thanks to Alyson Heller for her amazing editorial input, and to everyone at Simon & Schuster.

Thanks to my parents, Pam and Tom Carroll, for always believing in me, and being a safe place for me. A heartfelt thanks to everyone who read drafts of this book and offered encouragement or advice: Lisa Allen, Nancy Winkler, Doug and Sarah Coleman, and to my critique group at Inspire Christian Writers. To Bryan Allen, who pushed me to submit my work. I appreciate you all so much!

This book would not be what it is without the help of Nancy Butts, an incredible writing instructor. A special thanks to Nancy and Gerry Winkler, for their willingness to let my boys play at "Nana's and Papa's," when I had a deadline to meet. Thanks to Ruth and Steve Gallo, Jason and Kristen Hickey, and Cory and Farah Lundquist, for their generous tech support.

To my Journey Girls, and my friends and family who

have supported me, I am so thankful to have you in my life. To God, my creator, and the author of every good and perfect gift, and to my husband Ryan, who makes me feel like a princess. To my wonderful two sons, Noah and Thomas: It is an honor to be your mom.

Chapter 1

✵ ✵ ✵

Once there was a girl with hair the color of
dead leaves, teeth the size of piano keys,
freckles as big as polka dots, and eyes that
couldn't see squat. Everyone laughed at her
and called her Polka Dot. Poor Polka Dot felt
like a *total* weirdo, and always wished a fairy
godmother would appear and cut her some slack.

But that was just too darn bad, because fairy
godmothers only care about beautiful girls
with wicked stepmothers. So when Polka Dot

spotted a fairy godmother resting on a park bench, she kept her wish simple and begged for better eyesight. Sweet naive Polka Dot, no one ever told her some fairy godmothers have ginormous attitude issues.

"I'm on a coffee break, kid," said the fairy godmother. "Get yourself some glasses and stop pestering me."

"Could you please stop writing in the car and talk to me?" Mom asked, flicking the turn signal and heading into the left lane.

"There's nothing to talk about," I answered, putting the finishing touches on my new story, "Polka Dot and the Cranky Fairy Godmother." "I don't want glasses. People who wear glasses get made fun of."

"Callie, we've been over this already. Your headaches are happening for a reason. It could be that you need glasses. A vision test won't take that long."

"You're right, it won't." I closed my journal and tucked it under my seat. No way was I showing up to Pacificview Middle School—my new prison, as of tomorrow—with nerd-tastic glasses on my face. With my freckles and crazy-frizzy hair, it would be like painting a target on my face and handing out bows and arrows to the student body. So last night, I'd come up with a plan—a way to make sure I didn't get stuck wearing glasses, no matter how bad my eyesight was.

I shifted in my seat and looked at Mom. "Dad said I should get contacts instead of glasses."

Mom's lips stretched so thin they practically disappeared. "If your father were around—other than via his cell phone—maybe we could afford contacts. But he's not."

"Mommy, when's Daddy coming home?" Sarah, my four-year-old sister, asked from the backseat.

Usually when Mom kicked Dad out only a couple of weeks passed before they made up. But he'd been gone for a month already. He was staying with a friend up in northern California until they worked things out.

"Mommy's not sure," Mom answered.

Sarah started singing to herself, and Mom and I were silent. These days it seemed like if we weren't fighting, we didn't have much to say to each other. Our conversations were usually limited to arguing about chores or exchanging phone messages. I thought about holding my breath until she asked me something—like how I was feeling about starting seventh grade, or if there were any boys I liked— but I figured I'd pass out first.

Mom turned the car into a weathered strip mall. Squished between a dry cleaners and a doughnut shop was a tiny store with the word OPTOMETRIST painted in white block letters across darkened glass.

"It looks creepy. Are you sure we're in the right place?" I asked as we got out of the car.

"It's not creepy. And I need to pick up a few things for my classroom." Mom pointed to a teacher supply store on the other side of the dry cleaners.

Mom handed me a blank check. Then she took Sarah's hand and headed toward the supply store. I stared at the optometrist sign. I'd been to this strip mall a million times with Mom and never noticed an eye doctor's office before. Hadn't the dry cleaners been next door to the doughnut shop? And what was up with the tinted windows?

A small bell jingled when I opened the door, and the inside was seriously weird-looking. Heavy purple drapes hung behind red velvet couches in the cramped waiting area. Beaded lamps cast shadows on the walls. A single dusty display case housed a small selection of glasses frames.

A plump woman sat behind a large wooden desk. Thick glasses hung from a beaded chain around her neck. "Are you Callie Anderson?" she asked, smiling.

"Yeah."

"I'm Mrs. Dillard. Dr. Ingram is running late. Why don't you pick out some frames—just in case—and we'll finish up after your exam?"

I nodded and wandered over to the display case. After trying on several dorky-looking frames, I handed the least gross ones (caramel colored with rhinestones dotting the sides) to Mrs. Dillard. I tried not to think about all the weird looks I'd get if my plan didn't work and I had to actually *wear* them.

I did not want attention. I got nervous around people about as often as a mouse got nervous around a hungry cat. I didn't know why. Neither of my parents were shy. Mom taught fifth grade; Dad said she spent her days bossing people around. And Dad sold industrial vacuums to businesses and stuff like that; Mom said he spent his days turning on the charm. So who knew where my shyness came from? Maybe I was just a genetic mutant.

"Callie Anderson?" a male voice asked. I turned. A man with a shiny bald head and a bushy gray beard smiled at me. He wore a white overcoat and thick black glasses. "I'm Dr. Ingram. I apologize for the delay." He motioned to his office. "Follow me."

After I settled into the examination chair, Dr. Ingram

spent the next several minutes trying to blind me by flashing a white light into my eyes and asking me to blink.

"Do you like wearing glasses?" I asked.

"What, these?" Dr. Ingram tugged on his thick black frames. "Of course. They're quite useful. They help me see who merely needs eyewear and who requires vision correction."

"Aren't they the same thing?" I asked, but Dr. Ingram didn't answer.

"Excellent." Dr. Ingram switched off the light. "Your eyes seem quite healthy. Now we shall check your vision."

"I'm ready," I said, smiling. "Bring it on." I might have been a C-plus student (and that plus was only because of my A in English), but I knew how to study when it *really* mattered. Last night, I Googled the eye chart and memorized the whole thing—from the ginormous *E* at the top, to the microscopic *D* at the bottom. Twenty-twenty vision, here I come!

Dr. Ingram flipped a switch, and a projector turned on showing rows of increasingly smaller letters. But instead of the *E*, there was a *G* at the top. As I scanned the rest of the chart—the rows I could actually see, anyway— I realized the letters were completely different from the chart I memorized.

"Isn't there another chart we can use?" I asked. "Like maybe one that starts with an *E*?"

"Do you mean the one with an *E*, *F*, *P*? Followed by a *T*, *O*, and *S*?" Dr. Ingram asked.

"Yeah, that's the one. Except it's not an *S*, it's a *T*. There's no *S* on that chart." I clapped a hand over my mouth, realizing what I'd just said.

"You're very observant," Dr. Ingram said, grinning. "But I think we'll stick with this chart today."

"Oh, okay," I said, swallowing hard and wiping my sweaty palms on the leather seat.

Dr. Ingram quizzed me on the eye chart and my stomach knotted up like it always does when I take a test. And as the letters grew smaller, my answers grew unsure.

"Um . . . *Z*?" I said, squinting. "No, wait. *S*? No. *G*?"

"It's not a spelling bee," Dr. Ingram said kindly. "Though I'm sure you're quite competent in that subject. But alas, your vision is impaired. We shall have to find a suitable solution. I'm afraid you require glasses."

Dr. Ingram pushed a metal machine in front of my face. He loaded it with different lenses until I could read the bottom row of letters without squinting. Then he switched off the projector, and I started to rise from the exam chair.

"Not so fast. We've only begun to check your vision. We've still got quite a ways to go."

Dr. Ingram flipped the switch again. This time, instead of letters, I saw really funky black-and-white pictures. My dad, who liked to paint, would've said they were abstract.

"What's that?" I asked, pointing to a picture that looked like a spotted lump of nothing.

"You tell me," Dr. Ingram said. "There's no right or wrong answer. Tell me what you see. Better yet, tell me what that image reminds you of."

"Um, *okay*." I wondered if there was an answer that would get me out of his office without glasses. But after thinking about it for a minute, I decided to just tell the truth. "I see Charlie Ferris."

"You see Charlie Ferris?" Dr. Ingram repeated, raising two bushy eyebrows.

"Charlie Ferris, yeah. He used to tease me last year—and the year before that—and call me Polka Dot. Because, well, you know." I tapped my freckly cheek. "Almost everyone called me Polka Dot."

The next picture showed an image of what looked like a swan fighting off a dragon.

After I told that to Dr. Ingram he said, "And what does that remind you of?"

"Um . . . I guess it reminds me of my best friend, Ellen Martin. She's fearless. She wouldn't care if anyone made fun of her. Not like anyone would. She's really pretty. And really smart."

Dr. Ingram showed me a few more pictures. The last one looked like a group of stones on one side, and a larger, solitary stone next to a square object on the other side.

"I see Ellen making a bunch of friends at middle school. Then I see me"—I pointed to the larger stone—"reading a book or writing a story in my journal."

"Do you find that easier than making new friends?" Dr. Ingram asked.

I shrugged. "Books and journals can't make fun of you or call you names."

"I see." Dr. Ingram switched off the projector. "I think that's quite enough." He scribbled on a slip of paper. "Here. Give this to Mrs. Dillard and she'll take care of the rest."

"Whatever." I stuffed the paper into my pocket.

"Is something wrong?"

I stared at Dr. Ingram, and something in me snapped. I'd spent all summer dealing with thoughts about middle school the same way I dealt with chores, fights between my parents, and zits: ignore them and hope they'll just go away. But now those thoughts crashed into me like a tidal wave.

I wanted to tell Dr. Ingram all the things I couldn't say to anyone else. That I missed my dad, and wished he'd come home soon. That I felt nervous about starting middle school—especially since I'd gotten stuck with drama for my elective. How I worried that, just like elementary school, Pacificview would be a place where I didn't fit. How I felt like there was some all-seeing eye fastened on me—just waiting for me to screw up so everyone could laugh at me.

I wanted to tell him those things—but instead I said the same thing I told Mom whenever she asked me that question.

"Nothing's wrong. I'm fine."

Dr. Ingram peered at me through his thick black glasses and said nothing. He stayed silent for so long I thought he'd fallen asleep with his eyes open.

"Dr. Ingram," I said. "Are you—"

"Do you want to see?" Dr. Ingram interrupted. "I mean, *really* see."

"Uh, *yeah*," I said, confused. "That's why I'm here, isn't it?" *Duh*, I wanted to add but didn't.

"Wonderful. I'll be right back." Dr. Ingram disappeared through the door and returned a couple minutes later holding a small black case. "I spoke with Mrs. Dillard. Regrettably, there is a back order on the lenses we've selected. They should arrive in a few weeks—"

"That's okay. I don't really care when—"

"In the meantime, it just so happens I have a pair with your exact prescription that you may borrow." He opened the black case and held up what had to be the ugliest glasses in the entire world. They were huge. Their thick black frames looked like they'd survive a bomb blast. Actually, they looked a lot like the frames Dr. Ingram wore.

Except he wasn't wearing them anymore, I realized. Now Dr. Ingram's glasses were thin silver frames.

"Hey, weren't you just—"

"These glasses are very valuable." Dr. Ingram interrupted, placing them back in the case. "So please be careful."

"Okay," I said, thinking he'd probably tell my mom if I refused. "I'll take them."

I grasped the case, but Dr. Ingram didn't let go.

"You realize these are just loaners? You must return them when the time is right."

"When my other pair arrives, yes." Out in the waiting area the bell jingled, and I heard Mom ask Mrs. Dillard if I was almost finished.

"You're sure you want them?" Dr. Ingram asked. "You never know what you'll see when your vision is corrected."

"I'll take them, if you'll give them to me." I looked down at his hand.

Dr. Ingram let go. "Use them wisely, Callie."

"Of course I'll use them wisely," I said.

Whatever *that* meant.

Chapter 2

✳ ✳ ✳

Super Freaky Glasses Rule #1
*Don't get upset if someone secretly thinks
your glasses are ugly. They* **are** *ugly.*

PACIFICVIEW MIDDLE SCHOOL REMINDED ME OF A SCIENCE experiment gone wrong. A maze of gray metal lockers snaked in all directions, making me feel like a lost lab rat. Six hundred other rats also crowded the halls, some looking as nervous as I felt.

Ellen and I had been blessed with two classes together: math for first period and drama for seventh period. Just thinking about drama made me want to barf, but I figured I was really lucky to have two classes with my best friend.

I found my locker without too much trouble. After that, I needed to run an errand for Ellen. She wanted to join the yearbook club. Since my locker was closer to the English hall, she said it made more sense for me to pick up the application. Applications, actually—Ellen wanted me to join too. Ellen's goal was to throw herself into middle-school life. She thought we should join as many clubs as possible, which was a serious problem for me. Because my goal was just to survive middle school. By being as unnoticeable as possible.

Even if I didn't plan on joining any clubs, I was happy to pick up an application for Ellen—if I could just get my locker open. But after ten minutes of spinning, twisting, begging, and pleading with the attached combination lock, my locker sat smugly shut.

"What are you doing at my locker?" said a rough voice behind me.

I spun around. A pale-faced girl with midnight-colored hair glared at me. She wore all black. She also wore a dog collar. Really. Around her neck hung an actual dog collar, black with silver spikes.

"Um, well." Visions of getting stuffed in a trash can, locked in a janitor's closet, and a number of other scary images ran through my mind.

"I *said* what are you doing at my locker?"

"Th-this is my locker," I squeaked.

"No. It isn't." The girl shoved her locker assignment

slip in my face. "I've been assigned to three twenty-three. This is number three twenty-three."

"I know, but there's a shortage. So they had to double up on some of the lockers. It says so right here." I pointed to her slip.

She looked at the slip, rolled her eyes, and glared at me. "Mess with my stuff, and you'll be deader than the Doberman who used to wear this." She tugged at her dog collar necklace. Then she shoved past me and started spinning the lock. After five spins, three nasty words, and two punches, the locker finally sprang open.

While I waited, I fished my shaking hand into the plastic baggie in my jeans pocket and popped a couple of Red Hots (my favorite snack when I'm nervous) into my mouth. Then I unzipped my backpack and looked for my locker slip. Maybe by some miracle I was at the wrong locker, and I could just walk away from this angry girl.

My hand closed around my glasses case and I figured if there was ever a moment when I needed to see clearly, this was it. I put my glasses on, grabbed the locker slip, and noticed two things. The first was that the words were *a lot* sharper than when I read them earlier this morning without my glasses. The second was that the slip *did* say locker 323. Rats.

I popped a couple more Red Hots into my mouth. Their cinnamon smell didn't cover up the stinkosity of the hallway, which reeked of floor cleaner and sweaty gym socks.

Then something totally weird happened.

I'd heard about people hallucinating when they're stressed out, but this was worse. Way worse. All of a sudden, the air became wavy and shimmery, and computer screens the size of textbooks appeared out of thin air and hovered next to each student in the hall. Something that looked like a commercial played on one screen. On another, white words scrolled across a blue screen like those tele-prompters newscasters read from.

My mouth dropped open and I felt dizzy from staring at the screens. I stepped backward to get a better look, and collided with a group of students.

"Hey, watch where you're going!"

"Outta the way, Curly," said a boy who'd smacked into my shoulder.

"Don't you see the floating computers . . . ?" I said, staring at the strange screens.

"Move it," said my locker mate from behind me.

I turned around, and read the words scrolling across the screen hovering next to her:

Why is that four-eyed loser staring at me? I still need to find my class. At least it's just gym. No reading. I freaking HATE reading.

"How could anyone hate reading?" I asked, mesmerized by the screens.

Her gaze narrowed. "I didn't say I did. And what's the matter with you? Are you stupid or something?"

I stepped backward, bumping into even more students. Soon I was surrounded by a sea of people staring at me like I was captain of the freak squad.

Not that I could blame them. Normal people don't see floating computer screens in the halls of their middle school.

"Those glasses are, like, seriously geeky." I heard one girl whisper to another.

"Is everything all right?" A man who looked like a teacher waded through the crowd.

"What are your names, young ladies?"

"Callie Anderson," I said, while my locker mate answered, "Raven Maggert."

"Well, Callie and Raven, we don't want to start a fight on the first day now, do we?"

A screen appeared by the teacher's head and words scrolled across: *What horrid glasses. What were her parents thinking?*

It was the stress, I knew it. Middle school and my dorky glasses were a deadly combination.

"Anyway," the teacher was saying, "the bell is about to ring. I suggest you all move on and get to class."

"No problem." I slipped off my glasses, shoved through the crowd, and ran away.

First period hadn't even started yet, and already people thought I was a weirdo.

Ellen had her nose buried in a flyer listing Pacificview's extracurricular clubs when I arrived in math class. She didn't look up when I sat down. "What if we joined the hall monitor club?" she said. "We'd get to know a lot of people right away."

"Sure we would," I answered in a shaky voice. "They'd get to know us too—and run the other way."

I looked around the classroom, but didn't see any floating computer screens. Maybe if I took a few deep breaths and ate a few more Red Hots, I wouldn't have any more hallucinations.

"That's ridiculous. Only the slackers would run the other way." Ellen looked up then and frowned. "Are you okay? You look totally freaked out."

"I think I'm having a nervous breakdown."

"Will you stop with that?" Ellen said, sounding annoyed and going back to the flyer. "It's just middle school."

"No, that's not what I was—"

"And anyway," Ellen continued, "you can't spend another year hiding out with your journal. My mom says it's a new year and we should open ourselves up to new experiences."

"I don't care what your mom says. And I don't need new experiences," I said, thinking of the floating computer screens and the way everyone stared at me in the hall. "I like things the way they are."

That wasn't true. I didn't like things the way they were now. I liked them the way they were two months ago. During the first half of summer Ellen and I bodysurfed at the beach and had sleepovers at her house. We ate pizza and watched movies until Tara, Ellen's older sister, would leave for her dates. Then we'd sneak into Tara's room and read her diary.

Then in early August, Ellen went with her family to Yale—some college where my dad said the blood ran bluer than the Pacific—to get Tara settled for her freshman year. Ellen came home grouchy. I figured she just missed Tara. But every time I suggested we go bodysurfing or snooping in Tara's room she said I was being ridiculous. Everything seemed ridiculous to Ellen lately.

And I had a feeling she would think *I* was ridiculous if I told her I'd just seen computer screens floating through Pacificview's hallways.

"Hmm . . . there's a guitar club," Ellen said.

"*You'd* join a guitar club? Do you even own a guitar?" I didn't mean to sound all rude, but that didn't seem like a club Ellen would join—one that wouldn't win her any awards or look good on a college application.

Before Ellen could answer, a woman with wispy gray hair hushed the class. She introduced herself as Mrs. Faber and began to take roll.

"Calliope Meadow Anderson?"

"Present," I said, ignoring the giggles I heard whenever my full name was called. I glanced at the clock, and started to relax. I'd been in class for almost five minutes and hadn't had another hallucination. Maybe everything was going to be okay.

Or not. After roll call, Mrs. Faber went all drill sergeant on us and said she wanted to find out, and I quote, "how much mathematical data you retained over the summer, if any." So she passed out a practice quiz. Personally, I think that sort of behavior should be illegal on the first day of school.

I put my glasses on, stared at the test, and cringed. Because the amount of mathematical data I had retained over the summer was approximately zilch.

After the test, Mrs. Faber went over the answers and I

kept my head down. If I was seriously lucky, I answered two questions right. I skipped the other twenty-three. But Mrs. Faber seemed to have that special superpower that helps teachers zero in on students who are totally lost. "Could you tell us the answer to problem two, Miss Anderson?"

And then, it happened again.

As I looked up—about to give some bogus answer—the air waved and shimmered, and a screen appeared next to Mrs. Faber's head. Inside, blinking in bright pink neon letters, was the number twenty-nine.

I took my glasses off and rubbed my eyes, certain I was headed for the loony bin. But when I looked up and stared at Mrs. Faber, the screen had disappeared.

Quickly, I slipped my glasses back on. There it was: the screen next to her, with the number twenty-nine inside. I took my glasses off—the screen disappeared—and polished the lenses with the bottom of my T-shirt. Then I slipped them back on. The screen appeared again, the blinking pink twenty-nine inside.

So *I* wasn't a freak after all. My glasses were.

"Are you catching flies, Miss Anderson? Close your mouth. Now, does anyone *else* know the answer? Yes, Miss Martin?"

"Twenty-eight," Ellen said.

"No."

There was a gasp next to me—Ellen was probably shocked she'd actually gotten an answer wrong. Then a thought so fantastic occurred to me I nearly fell out of my seat. And I figured, *why not?* So I raised my hand.

"Yes, Miss Anderson?"

"Twenty-nine?"

"Yes, dear." Mrs. Faber smiled. "The answer is twenty-nine."

No. Freaking. Way.

The rest of class was the same. Mrs. Faber asked for an answer and I'd see a number on the screen hovering next to her. Whenever I took my glasses off, the screen disappeared. But as long as I kept them on I could see the screen that held the answers to Mrs. Faber's questions.

Maybe I was going crazy. But I figured if I was going crazy, I was going to do it in style. I raised my hand for every question, and when Mrs. Faber called on me, I had the right answer, courtesy of my super freaky glasses. Who knew having the answers could be so much fun? Not dreading it when the teacher called on you. No wonder Ellen raised her hand so much.

"And finally, number twenty-five?"

"Thirty," I called, and by this time my voice was confident.

The bell rang then and the rest of the class scurried off to second period. I gathered my things slowly, enjoying what was probably a once-in-a-lifetime experience.

Ellen cornered me as soon as I stepped out the door. "How did you know the answers?"

As Ellen asked the question, the air shimmered, and the screen appeared next to her. Only this time instead of numbers, there were words inside. Lots of words.

White letters scrolled across a blue screen: *There is no way on earth Callie could've known the answers to those questions. I bet she cheated off me. Maybe that's why she gets good grades in English. Maybe she's a cheater.*

"I am not a cheater!" A few students heading into Mrs. Faber's class turned and stared.

Ellen paled. "I never said you were a cheater."

The words on the screen changed: *Did I say that out loud? But she's right, I guess. Something's definitely up though. Callie stinks at math.*

"Did you pick up the yearbook club application for me?"

I blinked and tore my gaze away from the screen. "What? No. I got distracted."

Ellen expelled a puff of air, and the words in the screen changed again: *Figures. I swear, I should've just picked it up myself.*

I stepped back in surprise. Were the words on the screen Ellen's *thoughts*?

"Callie, are you okay? You're acting really weird."

"I'm fine," I said. I decided to perform an experiment. "What do you think of my new glasses?"

"They're nice," Ellen said.

But that's not what the screen hovering beside her said: *They're hideous. They make your eyes look huge and your teeth look even bigger than they already are.*

"You don't think they make my eyes look big?"

"Don't be ridiculous," Ellen said. But the screen said: *Yep, big as saucers.* "Look, I'm going to be late. I'll see you in drama, okay?" Ellen hurried off, and the screen beside her disappeared.

I stared after her, frozen. My glasses had magic powers.

They could read people's thoughts.

Chapter 3

✬ ✬ ✬

Super Freaky Glasses Rule #2
*Make sure your crush actually Knows Who
You Are before you spy on his thoughts.*

Trust me on this one.

SEEING THE THOUGHTS OF PACIFICVIEW'S STUDENT BODY
sent me crashing through the halls. Twice I bumped into a
group of angry girls, bringing me unwanted attention. As
I stammered out an apology, I saw their thoughts on the
screens hovering next to them:

*Look at that hair. Looks like she stuck her finger in a light socket. And
those glasses!*

Wow. Did she, like, steal her grandpa's glasses?

Is she a special ed kid? Maybe we should find her teacher.

My classes went okay, except I didn't understand a
word my Spanish teacher said—probably because she spoke

Spanish the whole time. Raven Maggert ended up in two of my classes, but otherwise the day was a haze of textbooks and the usual first day junk.

During class I experimented with my glasses and discovered that half the time, even my teachers didn't pay attention in class. My history teacher spent the whole period thinking about a baseball game he wanted to watch. In gym class Miss Riley barked at us to listen up and stop watching the boys' soccer practice—but she was actually thinking about some guy she liked.

Which weirded me out. My mom is a teacher so I know they have their own lives. But I still like to believe that *my* teachers are basically the opposite of vampires. At dusk they crawl into a hole and don't come out until first period.

As I was walking to fifth period, I saw a really cute boy looking at me. It made me feel sort of fiustered, but sort of happy. Until I read his thoughts: *Nerd alert, nerd alert, nerd alert!* We walked into class together, and he took a seat as far away from me as possible.

Apparently my glasses had another magic power: They repelled boys.

Throughout the day as I read the strange blue screens, I wondered *why* I'd been given a pair of magic glasses. Dr.

Ingram told me to use them wisely. Did he know there was something special about them?

I was still wondering when I arrived at drama, the last class of the day. A sign on the double doors read **MULTI-PURPOSE ROOM**, in stenciled black paint. And below that a handmade sign welcomed students to Mr. Angelo's drama class.

Just open the door and walk in, I commanded myself. But my arms and legs weren't taking orders at the moment. So I continued to stand in front of the door, paralyzed.

The thing was, I never would have signed up for drama. When we had opened our class schedules and I saw drama listed, I was sure there had been a mistake. Until Ellen told me that on orientation day last spring she crossed out "art" on my elective slip and wrote "drama" instead. Guess I should've been suspicious when she offered to turn the slip in for me.

"I didn't think it was that big a deal," Ellen said, all blond-haired and blue-eyed innocence. "I just wanted to make sure we had a class together. Please Callie? Do this for me?" Ellen held out her pinky. "Best friends forever?"

If having a class together was so important to Ellen, she could've changed *her* elective choice and taken art with me, I had wanted to say.

But I couldn't do it. "All right," I had mumbled instead, and crossed my pinkie with hers in our usual pledge. "Best friends forever."

Now I felt around in my pocket for my plastic baggie and popped some Red Hots into my mouth. If I had been given a pair of magic glasses, why couldn't they do something *really* cool, like make me invisible?

"Could you move?" said a rough voice behind me. "You're blocking the door."

I turned around. Raven stood in front of me, looking just as sullen as she had in English.

"Hi, Raven," I said, moving aside.

"Are you deaf, or what?"

"What?"

"Our locker is totally trashed—I *told* you not to mess with my stuff."

"Oh, s-sorry. I was putting my stuff away and then things fell out and then—"

"Whatever." Raven held up her hand. "Like I said, stay away from me, and stay away from my stuff." Raven stepped around me and slunk into the multipurpose room.

I followed her. Rows of folding chairs faced a darkened stage, where a thin red carpet ran from front to back. It reminded me of a large, toothless mouth, ready to swallow me if I set one foot on that monster. Off to the side, a portable whiteboard stood with a message scrawled in blue marker:

The seventh-grade class will perform CINDERELLA in December. Tryouts are in two weeks.

Okay, so *Cinderella* was definitely my favorite fairy tale. Something about her story gave me a hopeful feeling. Maybe it was the dress, or the ball, or the pumpkin carriage. But still, reading the whiteboard made me want to run out the door, down the hall to the principal's office, and request a schedule change. Why in the world had I agreed to stay in drama?

Because Ellen asked you to and she's your best friend, I reminded myself as I walked down the aisle. That's what best friends do.

Raven plunked down in a middle row. I didn't want to sit anywhere near her, so I chose a row toward the back and placed my backpack beside me to save Ellen's seat.

More kids quietly slipped inside, until the door burst open and Ellen bounded in, followed by a girl with golden skin and hair. I waved at Ellen. But Ellen was too busy talking and giggling with the Golden Girl to notice.

Everyone turned to watch Ellen and the Golden Girl as they trooped up the aisle, and I felt a familiar feeling—like something was coiling around my chest and squeezing tight. Jealousy. Not that I wanted people watching *me*—but sometimes it was irritating having a best friend who was really smart *and* really pretty. Wasn't there a rule somewhere that said you could be one or the other, but not both? And how come I didn't get to be either?

I studied Ellen's new friend. She kept giggling and tucking her hair behind her ears as she sashayed up the aisle. She reminded me of when Sarah dressed up in Mom's clothes and pranced around, just waiting for someone to tell her she was beautiful.

"Hey, look," she said loudly, "there's Raven."

Raven turned, and I saw her face pucker like she had just sucked a lemon. But Ellen and her new friend didn't seem to notice; they plunked down next to Raven and began whispering to her.

Ellen knew Raven? And who was the Golden Girl? And most important, why hadn't Ellen looked for me?

"Excuse me?" an accented voice said above me.

I looked up. A girl with mocha-colored skin and hair the color of coffee beans grinned at me. She seemed familiar, but I couldn't figure out why.

She smiled and looked right at me as she pointed to the empty seat and said, "May I sit there?"

This was very different from the girl who asked me that same question in English class earlier. *She* had smiled half-heartedly, and looked at the door while she spoke. Like in a sea of unknown faces, she had weighed her options, and decided I might have potential. But, if someone else walked into class, someone with better hair, or better clothes—someone who looked like they might one day become middle-school royalty—then she might change her mind.

But *this* girl continued to smile right at me as she repeated her question.

"Sure," I said, snapping back to attention and moving my backpack.

"I think my uncle lives next door to you," she said, sitting down. "Esteban Garcia? I just moved here from Mexico—he said I could come live with him. My name is Ana," she said, pronouncing it like *Ahn*-a.

"Okay." I *had* seen Ana before—in the front yard while the two Garcia boys chased each other with squirt guns. At the time, I just thought she was their new babysitter.

"I'm Callie."

"I've seen you in your window, writing," Ana said. "Did you have school in the summer?"

"Summer school? No, I just like to write. Stories and stuff like that."

Ana looked impressed. "I love stories. You must show me yours sometime."

"Sure," I said. Ana settled in and I looked at the front row again.

I felt stumped as I watched Ellen—like I was staring at a puzzle with missing pieces. How had Ellen managed to make a whole new group of friends in the last six hours? I slipped on my glasses, waited for the screens to appear, and then stared at the Golden Girl's thoughts.

At first there was an image on the screen hovering next to her—a picture of a pudgy girl with dull blond hair and green rubber-band braces. Then the screen changed and words scrolled across: *I can't believe I have two new friends already! I love science class! How awesome is it that we can all be lab partners? Don't be an idiot, Stacy, and forget their names: Ellen Martin and Raven Maggert. Ellen Martin . . .*

Okay, so Ellen had science class with Raven and Stacy the Golden Girl. So what? I sat with two other kids in science class too. That didn't mean I was going to suddenly start ignoring my best friend.

I looked at the screen hovering by Raven: *I can't believe these morons are my lab partners.* Then Raven glanced at Ellen and smirked: *Maybe I could get the uptight one to do most of the work.*

I grinned and turned to Ellen's screen, expecting to see a ton of thoughts about how middle school totally rocked: *I am sick of all these ridiculous classes! What's the point? If I do well, I'll just end up at Tara's stupid college anyway. I am so tired of hearing how wonderful Tara is. And why won't Mom and Dad let me get a guitar? It's not like I'm going to start a punk band or something.*

What? Those couldn't be Ellen's thoughts. I took my glasses off and banged them against the chair in front of me, like a flashlight with dying batteries. But when I put them back on and the screen appeared by Ellen, her thoughts were the same. I took my glasses off again and polished them with my T-shirt.

Just then I noticed a boy sitting a couple of rows ahead of me. His shaggy brown hair was pulled back into a short ponytail. My mouth dropped open and my heart started doing jumping jacks. Scott Fowler was in my drama class! I watched as he spoke to the boy next to him—who, I realized with a sinking feeling, was Charlie Ferris.

Last year, Scott Fowler was the cutest boy in the sixth grade. And I would know. I spent large chunks of classroom time staring at him and his ponytail. Ellen said his ponytail made him look scruffy and unhygienic, but I thought he looked mysterious, especially with his usual smirk, like he knew something no one else did.

When we studied poetry last spring, Scott wrote the most romantic haiku I'd ever heard. I even copied them into my journal, which Ellen thought was lame. "It's not like he wrote them for you, specifically," she'd said. But I didn't care. In the stories I wrote about Scott, I pretended he did write them for me—right before he confessed his undying love.

Just then Scott looked over. Our eyes met and my face flamed up like I'd crunched a gazillion Red Hots. As I quickly slipped my glasses back on, my thoughts were clear. Last year, I would've given anything to know what Scott thought of me. And right now, I could find out. I held my breath as the air waved and shimmered and the screen appeared next to him: *Dude, those glasses are epic ugly. Wait, isn't that Polka Dot? Ellen Martin's best friend? What was her name . . . Carrie, maybe? The one who never talked.*

Scott gave Charlie a nudge and pointed at me. A screen launched up next to Charlie as he turned: *Hey, it's Polka Dot! I knew I saw her in Spanish class!*

I looked away and sniffed, causing Ana to ask, "Are you all right?"

"I'm fine," I mumbled.

But really, I wasn't sure what I should feel more upset about:

1. That Scott thought my glasses were "epic ugly."
2. That Scott remembered "Polka Dot," but thought my real name was "Carrie."
3. That Ellen hadn't looked around to find me, not even once. Now that she'd found Stacy the Golden Girl, it was like she'd forgotten about me completely.

Chapter 4

✫　✫　✫

Super Freaky Glasses Rule #3
Most people tell little white lies.
Don't get offended. You do the same thing.

WHEN THE BELL RANG, STUDENTS BURST FROM CLASS LIKE soda from a punctured can. I hung back and waited for Ellen, who was talking to Stacy.

"Callie, *there* you are," Ellen said, like she'd been looking for me.

"I was sitting behind you the whole time."

"I didn't see you. I figured you were late. Like usual."

Then why didn't you save me a seat? I wanted to ask but didn't. Instead I said, "I looked for you in the cafeteria." My stomach rumbled then, reminding me that when I couldn't find Ellen, I decided to skip lunch. So

I'd fled the crowded cafeteria and hid out in the library till the bell rang.

"I looked for you, too," Ellen said. But then the air shimmered and the screen appeared. Inside I saw an image of Ellen and Stacy laughing and eating sandwiches in the cafeteria. I blinked, confused. What did it mean when the screen showed images, instead of words? Did it mean Ellen and Stacy ate lunch together? Was I seeing one of Ellen's memories?

Ellen introduced me to Stacy—Wanamaker—and explained they had four classes together, drama making it five. Then she turned to Stacy. "And this is Callie Anderson."

"I'm Ellen's best friend," I added quickly.

Stacy's grin faltered, but then she said in a bright voice, "Nice to meet you. I like your glasses, they're way cute."

The air shimmered again, and a screen appeared by Stacy. And my super freaky magic glasses showed me she was a total liar: *Should I tell her those glasses are way dorky?* The screen changed, and an image appeared of the pudgy girl with braces Stacy had been thinking about earlier. Was that someone she knew? I wondered. And what was I supposed to do with a pair of magic glasses, anyway?

I'd had enough middle school for one day. Reading

the blue screens and wondering what it all meant tired me out. I wanted answers, and only one person could give them to me.

I said good-bye to Ellen and Stacy and turned away, but Stacy stopped me. "Do you take the bus?"

"No, I just live a few tracts over, on Butterfly Way. But—"

"No way. I live close by too." Stacy leaned forward, and I caught a whiff of overpowering vanilla body spray. "My mom could take you home—maybe you and Ellen could come over."

"No," I said, more forcefully than I intended. "Anyway, I'll see you guys later." I avoided looking at the screen hovering next to Stacy and sprinted home, my overstuffed backpack slamming against my back. Inside my house, I thumbed through the yellow pages, but Dr. Ingram wasn't listed.

A note from Mom leaned against the phone, letting me know she would be late picking Sarah up from the baby-sitter's so could I put the casserole in the oven at 4:30? And could I unload the dishwasher and fold the towels? And for just once, clean my room because it was a total disaster?

Figuring I had plenty of time, I tossed the note aside,

kicked off my flip-flops, and headed upstairs to my room. Mrs. Dillard had given me a receipt for my order. Dr. Ingram's phone number was probably on it.

I was right. "Callie, how are you?" Mrs. Dillard said. "Dr. Ingram said you might be calling."

"I bet," I mumbled.

"Good to hear from you," Dr. Ingram said, coming on the line. "How are those glasses working out? Seen anything interesting?"

"You could say that," I said, then paused. Should I tell him about my glasses' super freakiness? I thought he knew they had magic powers. But what if he didn't? What if he told my mom? Or worse, what if he thought I was a weirdo?

"I've seen lots of interesting things," I said finally. When Dr. Ingram remained silent, I added, "And I was wondering if you could get my other glasses any faster? I don't think I like the loaner pair."

"Oh really? And why is that?"

Now I was silent.

"How was your first day of school? Do you like your classes?"

"I guess," I answered. "Except I'm taking drama and I have to figure out how to avoid auditioning."

"Auditioning for what?"

"For *Cinderella*. Our class is putting on a play in December."

"Wait just a moment," Dr. Ingram said. "You mean to tell me, you have the opportunity to be Cinderella, and you're not going to take it? You're not even going to try out?"

"Not if I can help it, and I'd never try out for the lead, anyway. And that's not the point."

"Yes. Yes, Calliope, that's absolutely the point," Dr. Ingram said. "Anyway, you wanted to know when your glasses will come in and the answer is I don't know. I'm afraid this is going to take much longer than I originally thought."

Dr. Ingram said good-bye and hung up. For now at least, I was stuck with the magic glasses. But what was I supposed to do with them? Even if I used the glasses wisely, wouldn't that be spying on people's thoughts? Was that even legal?

Outside my window I saw Ana walking down the sidewalk and carrying a stack of textbooks. I decided to perform one more experiment. I slipped my glasses out of the side pocket in my backpack and put them on. Then I jogged down the stairs and out the front door.

"¡Hola!" I said, using the one Spanish word I knew (other than *taco* and *enchilada*) as I met Ana on the sidewalk.

The cement was hot on my bare feet, and I hopped from one foot to the other, before stepping back onto the grass.

"*¡Hola!*" Ana answered, laughing. "Hello."

"So . . ." I thought carefully before asking my question. "What did you think of drama?"

"It was good," Ana said. The air shimmered and the screen launched up. Words scrolled across, but I couldn't understand any of them—they were all in Spanish.

"How did you like Pacificview?" I asked, trying again.

"It was good," Ana repeated. The screen changed, and what looked like a commercial began to play. A group of girls hanging out by a row of lockers laughed and pointed at Ana, who looked away and pretended not to notice.

Did that actually happen to Ana earlier? I wondered. Then I looked at Ana. Really looked. At her turquoise stretch pants and hot pink T-shirt. And I realized no one, not even someone as beautiful as Ana, could wear something like that to Pacificview and not catch grief.

Maybe the way I looked at her tipped her off, because Ana glanced at her clothing and said, "Is something wrong?"

"Well, it's just that your clothes are really . . . colorful. A little on the funky side."

"Funky? What does 'funky' mean?"

"Um, different?"

"And different is bad, yes?"

"No. Well, sometimes, I guess. Especially in middle school."

"Ah, you are giving me—what did my English teacher call it? A good cultural tip." Ana took a flyer out of her pocket. "My teacher also gave me this." She held it up for me to see—it was the same flyer Ellen had pored over earlier in the day. "There are a few clubs she thought I might want to join." Ana smiled widely and her eyes seemed to sparkle. "I'm going to show this to Tío tonight."

"Cool," I answered, trying to sound enthusiastic. Was I the only person in the entire seventh grade *not* excited about middle-school life? Everyone else at Pacificview seemed eager to join this club, or try out for that team. In gym class earlier I heard a couple of girls talking about soccer tryouts. One girl was just *dying* to be the goalie. But I didn't get it. Diving in front of a ball that was kicked by a girl with calves the size of Colorado did *not* seem like fun.

The screen hovering beside Ana changed then, and Spanish words began to scroll across. "How was your day?" she asked, shifting her textbooks from one arm to the other. The tone of her voice made me think it was the second time she asked.

"My day? Oh, yeah, no—it was good too." So far, my test wasn't going that great. I still didn't know how to use my glasses. I just knew Ana's day had probably been harder than she let on.

"So, how come you wanted to come to America?" I asked, changing the subject.

"My mother always wanted me to learn English very well. So I studied a lot. Then *mi tío*—my uncle—said I could come live with him to get an American education.

"Also." Ana paused. She seemed to struggle with what to say next, but then squared her shoulders like she'd made some kind of decision. "My father is sick."

"Sick?"

"*Sí*. Yes."

Ana told me about her family. They lived in an apartment in Mexico City. One morning, her father couldn't button his shirt—his hands were shaking too hard. Ana's mother helped him with the shirt, and he continued his day, selling newspapers on a street corner. But as the weeks passed, his hands shook harder. Soon after, he was diagnosed with multiple sclerosis.

It became harder and harder for Ana's father to work, and Ana's mother, who earned money by taking in laundry and cleaning apartments in the city, tried to increase her workload. Ana began missing school to sell newspapers, or to clean houses with her mother. When Mr. Garcia offered to let Ana come live with him, her parents thought it was an answer to their prayers. Ana had another relative in southern California—her aunt, Rosa. Aunt Rosa also offered to take Ana into her home, but Mr. Garcia insisted, saying he had a bigger house, and that it might be nice for Ana to get to know her younger cousins. He even offered to send Ana's parents money.

At first Ana spoke haltingly, but once she got going, the story just sort of flowed out of her, like she'd wanted to talk to someone for a while. Ana's English was good, and I gave up trying to understand the Spanish words scrolling on the screen next to her. If there was a word she didn't know in English, we just kept talking until I figured out what she meant.

"*Mi madre*—my mother—asked Tío if there was anything they could do to say thank you," Ana said.

"Was there?" I asked.

"*Sí.* He said maybe I could—what's the word?—kidsit?"

"You mean, babysit?"

Ana nodded. "Babysit. Yes, he said maybe I could babysit my cousins for him. I don't mind, my cousins seem nice."

While Ana spoke, the screen hovering near her changed. The Spanish words were replaced by an image of Ana trying to break up a fight between the two Garcia boys.

"Very nice," Ana repeated.

Ha! I was pretty sure I'd learned my first lesson: Those mini-commercials playing on the screen probably *were* people's memories; Ana just didn't want to tell me what a pain her cousins were.

"I should go," Ana said, pointing to her house.

"Okay," I took my glasses off. "See you in drama tomorrow."

I liked talking to Ana, I realized as I headed back to my house. It was the most real conversation I'd had with someone all day. About something that mattered, past the usual, "Hey, how are you?" Which, the glasses had showed me today, no one ever answered honestly.

Chapter 5

✵ ✵ ✵

Super Freaky Glasses Rule #4

List of things your magic glasses can't do:
homework, chores, or fix parent problems.

LATER THAT NIGHT, I WAS IN THE DOGHOUSE. I FORGOT TO put the casserole in the oven so dinner was late. Afterward, Mom sent me upstairs to do homework and then my chores (which I'd also forgotten about) before bedtime.

I sat cuddled up on my window seat. My bulging backpack sat next to me, but instead of doing homework, I stared at the star stickers on my ceiling, the kind that glow in the dark when you turn the lights off. I loved my room. I even had a name for it—the Meadow, after my middle name.

When I turned ten, my dad took three days off work so we could transform my room. We painted the walls yellow, and then painted a mural of a field of daisies on the wall across from my bed. We put in green carpeting and my dad bought me orange and brown throw pillows. I liked to scatter the pillows on the floor and pretend they were newly fallen leaves. Ellen thought the carpeting was, and I quote, "disgustingly hideous," which was about what Mom said, but Dad said it was romantic.

I unzipped my backpack and groaned. But then I had the most wonderful thought. What if my glasses had other super freaky powers I hadn't discovered yet? Like . . . what if they showed me the answers to my homework? Quickly, I pulled out my history worksheet, and looked for a question with an easy answer. Halfway down, I found one.

"In what year was William the Conqueror crowned king of England?"

I slipped on my glasses and stared hard at the question, willing a screen to appear. But after a few minutes I gave up. Apparently my super freaky magic glasses weren't going to do my homework for me. Rats. That meant *I* actually had to do my homework. Double rats.

But it could wait. I packed away the worksheet and slid my journal out from under the *Cinderella* script Mr. Angelo had passed out earlier. I still wondered why Dr.

Ingram gave me a pair of magic glasses. So I did what I
always do when I'm confused: I wrote a story.

Cinderella and the Stupid Prince

On the night of the grand ball, a fairy
godmother visited Cinderella. Besides the killer
dress and the pumpkin carriage, she gave
Cinderella a pair of magic glasses that could
read people's thoughts. When Cinderella realized
the Prince had fallen for her, she put them on
and waited breathlessly, ready to see what royal
thoughts would pour forth. But man was _she_
disappointed. Because the Prince, other than
thinking Cinderella was totally hot (and that her
glasses were totally not), didn't have a whole lot
going on upstairs, if you know what I mean.
Cinderella ditched him, leaving behind a glass
slipper. When the Prince's men came to her
stepmother's house, Cinderella locked herself in
the attic so they couldn't find her.

My door flew open just as I finished. "What are you doing?"
Mom asked.

"Would it kill you to knock?" I grabbed my script, hoping it looked like I was studying.

"Why haven't you done any of your chores?" Mom leaned against the doorjamb with her arms crossed, a frown on her face.

"You said I had to do them before I went to bed," I pointed out. "You didn't say *when* I had to go to bed."

Mom breathed deeply and closed her eyes, like she was meditating or something. When she opened them she spotted my journal.

"Have you been writing in that thing again? Don't you have homework?"

I hesitated before answering. It has always been my opinion that when you think you're about to get in trouble, play it safe. Play dumb.

"I don't know. I don't think so."

"You don't know? You don't think so?" When Mom got really mad, she repeated everything like it was a question. "You mean you don't remember? Get out your planner. You're not writing another word in that journal of yours, young lady, until—"

The phone rang then. By Mom's irritated voice, I knew my dad was on the other line.

"No, Nathan, I will *not* put Sarah on the phone. . . .

Because she's sleeping, that's why. If you want to talk to her, call back at a decent hour tomorrow. . . . Your muse? Not that again."

My dad liked to paint, and was always searching for something he called his "muse." And his muse must be pretty picky, because she'd told him a number of times to quit jobs he had held over the years. Like a Realtor ("I'm not asking some poor sap to mortgage his soul for a two-car garage and a granite countertop"); or a house painter ("I'm tired of painting white walls different shades of white"). Last month he said selling vacuums sucked the life out of him. I thought it was funny. But Mom didn't. She kicked him out of the house.

I motioned to Mom to give me the phone. If anyone would understand about my glasses, my dad would. Maybe I could even tell him I'd found a muse of my own—not one that told me to paint pictures and quit jobs, but one that told me people's thoughts. He'd know exactly what I should do.

"Well when you find your muse," Mom was saying, "ask her if she could refrain from ordering ninety-dollar neckties. Our credit-card bill came today. Our budget can't afford your muse's taste."

A pause and then, "You know what? I can't talk to you right now. Callie's here and she wants to say hi."

Mom thrust the phone into my hands and stalked away.

"Hi, Daddy—Dad." For the longest time I'd called my dad "Daddy," but lately it seemed kind of babyish.

"Callie Cat! Have you written any stories about your poor old man?"

When I started writing stories, my dad starred in them all. Sometimes I'd write that he was a government spy, or the prince of a secret kingdom. He loved my stories. *He* never got mad at me for writing instead of doing my homework.

"A few. I also wrote one about Cinderella and a pair of magic glasses." I told him about the story I'd just finished.

"That's wonderful Callie Cat," Dad said. "Keep it up. You could be the world's next Hemingway."

"Thanks. I got the idea from my new glasses. You'll see them when you come down this weekend."

"Actually, that's why I called. I can't make it this weekend. Maybe the week after, okay?"

"Sure. But the glasses—"

"Yes, I know. Your mother told me how upset you were about getting them. How are you two getting along these days anyway?"

"The usual," I said, sighing. "She thinks I'm lazy and she doesn't like it when I write in my journal. I try not to let her know when I'm writing."

"Well what your mother doesn't know won't hurt her. You're an artist, just like your poor old man."

Dad went on to talk about a vineyard he'd visited in Napa, and how it inspired him to paint again. While he talked, I lost my nerve. His muse was a pretty field of grapes somewhere, not something magic. If I told him, and he thought I was a weirdo, he might say something to Mom. Which would totally tick her off. Then she'd be in an even worse mood than usual and be on my case constantly. And I decided I didn't need that.

"So, anything else exciting happen today?" Dad asked after I'd told him about Pacificview—minus my super freaky glasses.

"No. Nothing exciting."

"All right. Take care of yourself, Callie Cat. Love you lots."

"Love you lots too."

After I hung up, I grabbed my journal, and promised myself I'd start my homework as soon as I finished a quick story about my dad. My head was beginning to hurt, so I slipped on my glasses. A few minutes later, a sound near the door made me look up. Mom stood in the doorway, with a look on her face that told me I was *way* past just being in the doghouse.

The air shimmered and a screen appeared next to her. Inside was an image of Dad as he painted in our garage. Mom stood behind him, talking and looking irritated.

"I told you," she said in a low voice, "not to write another word in that thing."

"Dad thinks I'm an artist," I said softly, staring at the screen. "Just like him."

"That's exactly what I'm afraid of." Mom strode into the room, snatched my journal away, and left.

I stared after her, wondering about the image I'd just seen. When Mom looked at me, did she see my dad?

Reluctantly, I hefted my textbooks out of my backpack and settled them on my window seat. I looked outside at Ana's house. I wished my magic glasses could've teleported me over there. Because right then I figured Ana was probably having more fun in her house than I was in mine.

Chapter 6

✷ ✷ ✷

Super Freaky Glasses Rule #5
If you think you're about to make a complete fool of yourself, take the glasses off.

As the days passed, I learned how to wear my glasses without bumping into people, crashing into walls, or turning into a weirdo in general. Oftentimes when I spied on people's thoughts, the glasses showed me images instead of words: memories or daydreams. Sixth period was a great time to spy on people's daydreams—right after lunch, no one ever paid attention to the teacher.

And most of the time, people never said what they really thought.

Me to a girl in first period: "How are you?"

Girl in first period: "Great." *What do you care? What does anyone care? I hate this stupid school.*

Me to a girl in second period: "That's a cute shirt. Where did you get it?"

Girl in second period: "Oh it's just something my dad bought on a business trip to Paris." *It's from Pacificview Thrift. Good thing Callie doesn't know anything about fashion.*

Me to a girl in third period: "Did you have a fun weekend?"

Girl in third period: "Totally! I saw Jacob Ryan at the mall on Saturday and we split a slice of pizza. He's such a sweetheart." *But why hasn't he called me back? He had to get my messages—I left, like, twenty of them.*

"Sometimes," a girl named Brandy answered in fourth period after I asked her if she got along with her parents. For the most part, her words matched the thoughts scrolling across the screen hovering near her.

The bell rang and we began gathering up our things. "It's been nice to talk," Brandy said. The words on the screen changed then: *Maybe Callie isn't stuck-up, after all.*

Me, stuck-up? I read the screen a second time. Was she serious? I wasn't stuck-up. Okay so maybe I never talked to Brandy—or any of the other girls, besides Ellen—last year in sixth grade. But it wasn't because I was stuck-up. It was because I figured they all thought I was a weirdo.

"You know," Brandy continued, slinging her book bag over her shoulder, "we went to elementary school together, and this is the most you've ever talked to me."

"Yeah, I guess it is," I said weakly, as we headed out of class and went our separate ways. I realized then that I'd been so busy experimenting with my glasses I forgot to be nervous when I talked to people.

But my nervousness came rushing back when I walked into drama later that afternoon. Auditions for *Cinderella* were today. In front of the stage stood a table with two sign-up sheets. One instructed us to sign up for a back-stage crew, like lighting or set decoration. The other was an audition sheet.

Normally I would've talked to Ellen before signing up, to find out what crew we were joining. But Ellen wasn't there yet, so I added my name and hers to the paint crew list, and skipped the audition sheet.

Ana was hunkered down in a corner, studying her script. She smiled and waved when she saw me. I wasn't sure if I should join her, so I plunked down by myself on the floor. Then I fished out my plastic baggie of Red Hots, popped a few in my mouth, and tried not to look like a loner.

Ellen and Stacy breezed in a minute after the bell rang.

After receiving a scolding from Mr. Angelo, Ellen plopped down beside me with Stacy following close behind, firmly wedging herself between Ellen and me. Which was totally irritating. Stacy was always *around*. Sitting with us in drama. Constantly hanging around Ellen's locker. This week she'd even started eating lunch with us.

"You need to sign up for an audition slot and a backstage crew," I said to Ellen.

"Could you sign me up, Callie? Please, best friends forever?" Ellen was too busy rummaging through her backpack to hold up her pinkie.

"Yeah, sign me up too," Stacy chimed in. "Ellen and I decided we want to try out as Cinderella, and we both want to work on costumes."

"But I already signed us up for the paint crew," I said to Ellen, ignoring Stacy.

"Don't be ridiculous." Ellen pulled her script from her backpack. "Painting's your thing, not mine."

After I finished with the sign-up sheets and rejoined Ellen and Stacy—firmly wedging myself between *them*— I noticed them staring at their scripts and trying to hold back laughter. Was I missing something?

Thanks to my super freaky magic glasses I could find out what was going on—I wouldn't even have to ask. I pulled them out from the side pocket of my backpack and slipped them on. The air waved and shimmered, and blue screens appeared by Stacy and Ellen.

Stacy: *Those guys were soooo cute; we should've talked to them more. Who cares if we're late to class? Ellen needs to loosen up.*

Ellen: *Tara never had a boyfriend in seventh grade. I wonder what it would be like . . .*

I almost choked on a Red Hot. Ellen never talked to, or about, boys. *I* was the one who got all wrapped up in a crush and wanted to talk about boys. Well, okay, so far I'd only liked two boys in my life: Dario Martinez in fifth grade and Scott Fowler in sixth grade. I glanced over at Scott, who sat with Charlie Ferris and studied his script. Yep, Scott was definitely a to-be-continued sort of story.

But Ellen getting all twittery over a boy? Forget it. A cat was more likely to get excited over a bubble bath. Ellen probably could've had a boyfriend by now, but she was usually too busy freaking out over school and her grades to care.

"So," I said to Ellen, trying not to grin too widely, "how come you were late?"

"Um," Ellen hesitated. "Stacy . . . Stacy couldn't get her locker open." Ellen went back to her script, and I read the one thought scrolling across the screen hovering next to her: *Callie wouldn't understand.*

"Oh." I felt a pain in my chest, like a bee had stung my heart. "Okay."

"Okay, what?" Ellen asked.

"Nothing."

It wasn't a big deal, right? If I'd been the one in the hall with Ellen she'd have been giggling about it with me. Except . . . except the glasses had shown me things about her I hadn't known. Ellen had a recurring daydream of herself rocking out with a guitar—even though when I *asked* her if she wanted to play an instrument, she told me not to be so ridiculous. And Ellen was obsessed with trying to be better than her older sister, Tara. In her mind it was always, *Tara this* and *Tara that.* I never realized how hard it was having a sister like Tara—someone who excelled at everything. (I figured Sarah should be grateful to have me for an older sister. Because, let's face it, so far in my school career I wasn't setting the bar all that high.)

Sometimes Ellen would think about telling me something—like the fight she and her mother had last week over guitar lessons—but she'd decide against it. *Callie wouldn't understand,* she'd think to herself. Then she'd stop talking.

Kind of like now.

Stacy wore a smug smile and the screen hovering next to her practically popped with fireworks: *Ellen didn't tell her!*

It's hard to believe they're best friends. Maybe Ellen will come over after school today again.

Again? When did Ellen hang out at Stacy's house?

"Callie?" Mr. Angelo said from the stage. "Can you come up here, please?"

"Sure." At that moment, walking away sounded like a great idea. I slipped off my glasses and headed over to the stage.

Mr. Angelo was my favorite teacher, even if his stringy blond hair reminded me of a bowl of limp spaghetti. He let us eat in class and sit on the floor, saying he didn't want something as elemental as chairs to hinder our "process." I didn't know what that meant, but it sounded good to me.

"Yes, Mr. Angelo?"

Mr. Angelo held up his clipboard. "Your name isn't on the sign-up sheet."

"Yeah, that's because I'm not auditioning. I'm a behind-the-scenes kind of girl."

"Be that as it may, students are required to perform onstage as well as contribute backstage."

"Sure, but"—I jerked my head toward Ellen and Stacy—"there are plenty of girls who want to audition. Besides, drama's really not my thing."

"Not your thing? My dear girl, one has not truly lived until one has set foot on the stage. And I shall not deprive you of the honor." Mr. Angelo dropped a script into my hands.

"Wait. This is for the lead. I don't want to be Cinderella."

"Callie," Mr. Angelo said exasperatedly, "every girl wants to be Cinderella."

Auditions began and it seemed Mr. Angelo was right. Maybe every girl really *did* want to be Cinderella. At least, that was the part most girls tried out for. Stacy was the giggliest Cinderella I'd ever seen, desperate to get the Prince's attention (although personally, I couldn't tell if she was acting or just being herself). One girl froze up onstage and could only mime dancing at the ball before she had to give up.

Raven tried out as the Fairy Godmother, glaring if anyone in the audience even sniffed during her audition. Ana made a regal Fairy Godmother—probably because she was trying hard to pronounce each word perfectly. Scott went next. He forgot a few lines as he strutted across the stage, but I didn't think it mattered. In my opinion, he was a perfect Prince.

"And next up," Mr. Angelo said, squinting at the sign-up sheet, "I can't read this. Mr. . . . I.P. Freely?"

The class burst out laughing and Mr. Angelo let out a long-suffering sigh.

"Here I am," said Charlie Ferris. "Freely is my code name. But you can call me Ferris. Charlie Ferris."

"All right, *Mr. Ferris*, you may begin."

Charlie seemed like a natural. He blew a kiss to an imaginary Cinderella and had the class laughing as he pretended to trip over a left-behind glass slipper.

"Why are you taking drama this semester?" Mr. Angelo asked when Charlie finished.

Charlie hesitated. Then he broke into a wide grin. "Easy A."

"Brilliant answer," Mr. Angelo replied, sounding like he didn't mean it at all.

Charlie shrugged and jumped off the stage, winking as he passed us.

"Did you see that?" Stacy said, nudging Ellen. "He just totally winked at me."

I rolled my eyes—Stacy's favorite topic of conversation seemed to be all the boys who noticed her each day.

When Ellen's turn came, my stomach knotted up like a cinnamon pretzel. But it didn't turn out to be quite so sweet.

Ellen chose the same scene Mr. Angelo handed me, and she had the graceful onstage thing down. But I never thought Cinderella was that confident, like she just knew her stepsisters were a bunch of hags, and she was destined to be a princess. Maybe it was just me, though; everyone clapped loudly after Ellen finished.

I put my glasses on and kept my head down after that, studying the script and trying to cram the lines into my head. The pretzel in my stomach wasn't going away; it squeezed tighter and tighter as my turn neared, threatening to make me barf up the Red Hots and corn dog I'd eaten for lunch.

"Are you okay?" Stacy asked when I started taking deep breaths.

"I don't think I can do this."

"Of course you can," Ellen answered. "I've seen you act out your stories. Drama is practically the same thing."

"Is not. And I do not act out my stories." Well, sometimes I did. But only in my room, and, since that time Ellen caught me, only with the door locked.

"Callie, you're up!" Mr. Angelo turned his head and beckoned me toward the stage.

I felt all eyes on me as I walked up the stairs to the stage. *Splat!* My flip-flop caught the last step and I went sprawling, head first, onto the stage. Stifled laughter wafted up from the audience below.

"Go, Polka Dot!" shouted a voice from the audience. Charlie Ferris, it sounded like.

"Ah, a comedic Cinderella," Mr. Angelo said. "I like it, continuing Mr. Ferris's use of physicality. Well done. Continue, please."

"Th-thank you," I stammered, pretending like I'd meant to fall. As I looked out at the audience, the air waved and shimmered. Screens launched up by every person in class and I began to read their thoughts:

Raven (slumped down in her seat and scowling): *Stupid drama. I can't believe Mr. Angelo called my mom. My attitude is fine. It's not my fault this stupid class reeks.*

Charlie (sitting with his head in his hands): *I know I screwed up. I should've spent more time practicing last night and less time hanging out with Scott.*

Scott (fidgeting in his seat): *This is such a waste. I told Charlie we didn't need to practice so much. Who cares about Cinderella anyway?*

Stacy (leaning forward): *Wow, she looks really scared. Is that part of her audition?*

Ellen (looking anxious): *Tara probably won't fly home for the play unless I get the lead. Mom and Dad probably wouldn't come, either. But I think I was better than anyone else—and Gretchen Baxter is the only one left, so hopefully I'll be Cinderella.*

Wait—what about me? I wanted to say. Gretchen Baxter was auditioning after *me*. Wasn't Ellen just a tiny bit afraid of the possibility, no matter how slight, that *I* might actually get cast as Cinderella? Not that I wanted to, but still.

"Whenever you're ready," Mr. Angelo said.

"Yes, sorry. I'm ready."

A little fear might do Ellen the Overconfident some good, I decided as I slipped my glasses off and tucked them in my back pocket. Mr. Angelo wanted a comedic Cinderella? Well, he was about to get one. I didn't know how to act. But I knew how to make people laugh at me. I stomped over to center stage and unleashed . . . *Klutzarella!*

First, I pretended to accidentally squash a friendly mouse with my new glass slippers. Then, when I spun around in my huge new ball gown, I pretended to take out a coachman. Then I pretended my hair snagged on my new diamond tiara. And *then . . .*

And then, something happened. As I stuttered out my lines—about how grateful I was to my fairy godmother—I forgot where I was. I thought about Cinderella. A girl who was never seen. A girl who probably had so many talents, but no one ever knew. All they ever saw were her stepsisters. She might even have missed the ball because no one ever saw her. No one believed she was princess material.

"Okay, Callie. That's good," Mr. Angelo called from the front row.

That was it? Had I even finished my lines? The audience was silent, and everyone stared at me like they didn't know who I was.

Had I really been *that* bad?

If I really wanted to know how I did, I could've put on my glasses and read everyone's thoughts. But I didn't want to see that the entire class thought I'd choked.

Although, I thought as I walked off the stage, if I'd been really horrible, maybe Mr. Angelo would let me off the hook, and I wouldn't have to be in the play at all.

Chapter 7

✿ ✿ ✿

Super Freaky Glasses Rule #6

Don't wear your glasses at the dinner table. Spying on people's thoughts while they're eating is as rude as chewing with your mouth open. Plus, it makes you nauseous.

Pacificview Drama Class Final Cast List

Cinderella . . . . . . Callie Anderson

Prince Charming . . . . . . Charlie Ferris

Fairy Godmother . . . . . . Ana Garcia

Wicked Stepmother . . . . . . Stacy Wanamaker

Wicked Stepsister No. 1 . . . . . . Raven Maggert

The rest of the penciled-in cast list was a blur. I took my glasses off, hoping this was some kind of super freaky glasses trick. But when I looked at the list again, my name was still at the top.

Mr. Angelo said he wanted to talk to me before he posted the cast list. I thought he wanted to let me down gently, and tell me I should transfer into a different elective. I'd been smiling when I walked into drama ten minutes early.

I wasn't smiling now.

"You're kidding, right?" I said, handing the clipboard back to Mr. Angelo. "Right?"

"No. You saw it correctly. I'd like *you* to play Cinderella." Mr. Angelo smiled widely, like he'd just handed me a bowl of cinnamon ice cream.

But it felt more like a bowl of confusion. With a seriously large side order of no-way-ain't-gonna-happen.

"I think there's been a mistake—I don't want any part, remember?" I said, slipping my glasses back on. "Especially not the lead."

"I thought you might feel that way," Mr. Angelo said, sighing. "That's why I asked you to come early. I would like you to play Cinderella. But frankly, you act as though the very idea of stepping on that stage makes you ill. I don't understand why. I think you're quite talented, and your audition was amazing. . . ."

While Mr. Angelo complimented my great talent, a blue screen sprang up next to him, fast as Pinocchio's lying nose, and showed me he wasn't being totally honest: *A klutzy, fumbling Cinderella. I love it. I bet it's never been done. And she's a fairly competent actress to boot. Principal Reynolds thinks he's going to cut drama's budget next semester? I'll give him such a great fall show he'll have to eat his words.*

"But I won't give the lead to someone who doesn't truly want it," Mr. Angelo was saying. "So I'm offering you a choice: You can be Cinderella or, you can be Cinderella's understudy."

I looked down at the cast list. Ellen had been cast as Cinderella's understudy. My understudy. I had to admit, something about that sounded strangely good, but also strangely weird. Like I was living in some kind of alternate universe. But then reality came knocking.

I pictured myself standing onstage. In front of a whole auditorium full of people. Even if Mr. Angelo thought my fumbling klutziness was funny, I knew there were so many ways I could screw things up for everyone. I wished I'd kept Klutzarella to myself. Ellen really wanted the lead. What would it mean to our friendship if she had to be my understudy all semester?

For some reason, Stacy's face came into my head just then. And as I scanned the rest of the list, I realized Scott had been cast as the Prince's understudy. Would I get to practice with him a lot if I was Cinderella's understudy?

"The choice is yours, Callie," Mr. Angelo said.

"I choose the understudy," I said, as students began wandering into class. "Let Ellen be Cinderella. She wants it more anyway."

"True enough." Mr. Angelo nodded, but he looked disappointed. With a flourish, he pulled a pencil from behind his ear. The eraser moved furiously across the clipboard, and soon there was a new list: Ellen Martin as Cinderella and Callie Anderson as Cinderella's understudy. Only a faint eraser mark showed the change.

I had a feeling Ellen wouldn't appreciate being second choice. I looked up at Mr. Angelo and said, "You won't tell Ellen about this, will you?"

Mr. Angelo grinned. "She'll never know."

"I thought your glasses were supposed to stop your headaches?" Ellen looked at me quizzically over the dinner table. Ellen had asked if she could come over to practice her lines. She'd spent most of dinner giving Mom and Sarah a minute-by-minute account of her audition, and stopped only when she noticed me rubbing my temples.

"They do. I'm fine." Or as fine as I could be—without letting on I could read everyone's thoughts. While Mom pretended to listen to Ellen, I knew she was actually waiting to ream me over the note she received from Señora Geck, which detailed my sorry performance in Spanish class.

And I knew that Ellen, who thanked Mom several times for the casserole we were eating (a strange concoction of corn, eggs, and spinach I thankfully remembered to put in the oven on time), secretly thought it looked like cat barf. Ellen was talking as much as she could to avoid eating it.

"Your glasses make your face look funny," Sarah said, giggling.

"Thanks, Sarah." Spying on Sarah's thoughts wasn't very interesting. She usually said exactly what she thought, including when she told Mom the casserole tasted slimy. I wondered at what age people learned to hide their true thoughts.

Ellen turned back to Mom. "And then Mr. Angelo said he'd never seen a Cinderella so sure of herself. He said he was counting on me to put on a great show for him." Ellen's voice was casual, but the screen hovering next to her showed a different story: *So what if Mr. Angelo thinks I need to work on "emotionally connecting" with Cinderella? He can be so flaky sometimes. It's Cinderella. What's there to connect with? Wait till I tell Tara and Mom and Dad. Tara never once acted in a play!*

I closed my eyes and rubbed my temples again. "Mr. Angelo is counting on you because if Principal Reynolds doesn't like the play he'll cut drama's budget next semester."

When I opened my eyes, both Mom and Ellen were staring at me.

"How do you know that?" Ellen asked. "Did Mr. Angelo tell you that?"

"That seems like an odd thing for a teacher to share with a student," Mom added.

"Um . . ." I trailed off, unsure what to say. Sometimes I really liked my glasses—like last week, when I read Stacy's thoughts and discovered she was about to invite me to shopping with her after school. I liked to avoid malls the same way I liked to avoid snakebites and bee stings—so I'd hurried out of drama class before she could ask me.

Other times I hated the glasses—especially when I read people's thoughts and discovered what they thought about *me*. More than one girl from my old elementary school thought I was stuck-up because I never talked to them. And I didn't know how to explain that it was because I was shy, not stuck-up.

And other times—like right now—it was a real pain

knowing everyone's thoughts but having to pretend like I didn't. If I told Ellen I had read Mr. Angelo's thoughts, Mom would have me seeing a doctor faster than you can say "crazy weirdo."

"I guess I must have overheard them talking," I said finally.

"Oh, okay," Ellen said, and then continued with her story.

Mom took a bite of casserole and smiled at Ellen, but her thoughts were still on me: *The semester's barely begun and she's already having problems. I'll have to get her a tutor—maybe Ellen can do it. Ellen has tutored her before.*

"Ellen's taking French this year!" I burst out, cutting off Ellen. Sarah giggled, but Mom and Ellen looked at me like I was a lunatic.

Mom didn't realize I'd been reading her thoughts; she jumped to her own conclusion. "So Señora Geck told you about the progress report, then? You know you need a tutor? And if Ellen can't do it then you've got to find someone else."

"Okay." I took a huge bite of casserole before I said something nasty. Why did Mom assume that Ellen was the answer to my problems? I couldn't wait for this weekend. Dad was coming to take Sarah and me on a "Daddy Date."

It would be nice to hang around a normal parent for a change. *He* wouldn't care about my Spanish grade.

"What time is Dad coming tomorrow night?" I asked.

"About that . . ." Mom paused—but the screen hovering next to her said it all. Inside was an image of her yelling at someone over the phone. It didn't take a genius to figure out my dad was probably on the other line.

"Your father can't make it this weekend," Mom said, looking down at her plate.

I grunted and took another bite of casserole. I wanted to tell Mom that if she'd stop screaming at Dad every time he called, maybe he wouldn't be staying away so long. But I couldn't. The thing was, I never told Ellen that Mom kicked Dad out. Not this last time—or any of the other times before. Sometimes I would want to tell her, but then I'd think about Ellen's parents, and how she told me they still held hands and how it embarrassed her—and then I just couldn't do it. So instead, I told her Dad was away because of work. Ellen always seemed to believe me, especially since Dad changed jobs so often.

"Are you okay?" Ellen asked me. *She looks upset,* read the white words scrolling across the blue screen hovering next to her.

"I'm fine," I said, and took another bite.

There was a silence, broken occasionally by the sound of scraping forks. Finally, in an overly bright voice, Ellen said, "If you're free then, want to go to the dance tomorrow night?"

"What dance?" I asked.

Ellen rolled her eyes. "Really, Callie, do you walk around school blindfolded? There are only a ton of posters all over campus. The Fall Dance. It's tomorrow night."

"Do you even have to ask? No way."

"Come on, it could be a lot of fun," Ellen said, but the screen next to her told me her thoughts were elsewhere: *Why are you even asking? You know she won't go. She's so selfish; she never does anything I want to do.*

I'm selfish? *I'm* selfish? I wanted to shout. What about all the things I did for Ellen? Like always meeting her at her locker before school started. Ellen never came to my locker, even though mine was closer to Mrs. Faber's class. Ellen always picked what we did. Like today—I wanted to stay after school with Mr. Angelo and the rest of the paint crew. But Ellen said we needed to practice our lines (translation: *her* lines) and couldn't be bothered with something as ridiculous as painting.

And, oh yeah, what about letting Ellen have the part of Cinderella in the first place. I'm selfish? Yeah, right.

But I couldn't say any of that. Instead I said, "I have absolutely no desire to go."

That wasn't exactly true. A small part of me really did want to go. The part that imagined me laughing and dancing in a big group of friends. But in my imagination I had frizz-free hair, a freckle-free face, and I knew how to make people laugh instead of worrying they were laughing at *me*.

In reality, if I went to the dance, I would stand awkwardly in a dark corner, drinking punch and trying not to look bored while one cute boy after another asked Ellen to dance.

"Are you sure you don't want to go?" Ellen asked. The words in the screen next to her changed then: *Maybe Stacy would go with me. She'd be fun to hang out with.*

I hesitated. Imagining Ellen and Stacy laughing it up all night was almost enough to make me change my mind.

Almost.

"I'm positive. And anyways"—I glanced at Mom—"I have a lot of homework due on Monday."

My words had the desired effect because Mom looked up and said, "Yes, Callie will need to stay in this weekend." *No way is she leaving this house without putting some serious effort into her Spanish.*

"See," I said to Ellen. "I can't go. Go ahead without me and have fun."

But not too much fun, I thought to myself. Not with that best-friend stealer Stacy Wanamaker.

After Ellen left, Mom went on and on about finding a Spanish tutor. Finally I told her I'd ask Ana. I looked down at my notebook paper as I rang the Garcia's doorbell. Usually Mom paid someone to tutor me. But I knew we couldn't afford that right now, so I'd ripped the story of "Cinderella and the Stupid Prince" out of my journal, hoping Ana would accept it as a gift.

Mom said since I was going over there anyway, would I ask Mr. Garcia if we could borrow a lightbulb? "The one in Sarah's room is burned out. And I completely forgot to buy one at the store today," she had said.

But I still had the glasses on, so I read her thoughts and knew she didn't forget. She just didn't have enough grocery money to buy one more thing—and she felt horrible for having to ask Mr. Garcia.

Mom got along with Mr. Garcia okay. Once he'd even helped her fix a flat tire on her car. I didn't like him, though, and the way he seemed not to notice when his sons shredded all the roses off my mom's bushes. But the day Sarah kicked a soccer ball and it accidentally bounced off his SUV, he lectured her about respecting other people's property.

No one answered the door. Reluctantly, I rang it again, wishing I could just go home. Last week, Mom sent me over to borrow some bread. Mr. Garcia had told me— twice—how happy he was to help someone in need.

The lock turned, snapping me back to attention. The door opened and Anthony Garcia, Ana's seven-year-old cousin, peered out at me.

"Hi, Anthony. Is Ana around?"

Anthony shrugged and walked back into the house. He left the door open so I followed him inside. He plunked down in front of the TV and hollered "Ana!" Next to him, Miguel, his four-year-old brother, played with Legos.

I heard keys jangling and turned to see Mr. Garcia walk into the hallway. Gray streaks peppered his dark hair, and lines etched his forehead. I remembered Mom telling me once that he'd married later in life—and then Dad adding that the reason Mrs. Garcia left was probably because she couldn't "put up" with Mr. Garcia anymore.

"Hello, Calliope." Mr. Garcia always called me by my full name. "How are you? I'm afraid we're all out of bread today."

"That's not why I came," I said, deciding I would use my allowance and buy the lightbulbs myself after school tomorrow.

Ana emerged from the kitchen then, wiping her hands on a blue apron she wore. Mr. Garcia said something to her in Spanish, which she answered by saying, *"No sé."* I was proud of myself for knowing that meant "I don't know" in English. Then both of them turned to stare at me.

Suddenly the already-crowded hallway seemed to shrink and I stepped backward, my hand closing around the doorknob. I wanted to fling the door open and run away from Mr. Garcia's snobby stare. I didn't want to tell him that—yet again—my family needed help from his.

But I forced myself to stay still while Mr. Garcia said, "I haven't seen your father's car in a while."

"Yeah, he's away," I said, hanging my head. "He's working."

"Oh, well that explains why the lawn looks the way it does. I could recommend a good gardener to your mother."

"That would be nice," I said. I didn't tell him there was no way we could afford a gardener right now. I turned to Ana. "So, I was wondering if you could help me learn Spanish. You don't have to, it's just that, my mom thinks I need help and I was wondering if you could tutor me." My words came out fast, so fast I thought Ana didn't understand me, because she said nothing. Instead she glanced uncertainly at Mr. Garcia.

"That's okay, I understand if you can't. See you at school." I turned around, and fumbled with the doorknob. Behind me I heard Mr. Garcia whisper something in Spanish to Ana.

"No, wait," Ana said. "You need help with Spanish?"

I turned back. "Yeah."

"Okay. *Le ayudaré.*" Ana said, and smiled. "That means, 'I will help you.'"

Mr. Garcia said good-bye to Anthony and Miguel and began talking to Ana in Spanish. While he spoke Ana nodded and said "*Sí.*" When he finished, he brushed past me and left.

"Where is he going?" I asked.

"He has to work, and he asked me to watch the boys." Ana paused and then said, "What's that in your hand?"

I looked down at the notebook paper clutched in my hand. I'd held it so tight it crumpled.

"It's just a story I wrote. I thought you might like to read it. You don't have to though," I added quickly. "It's probably not any good or anything."

Normally, I didn't show my stories to anyone except my dad. I was afraid Mom would get mad and take away my journal. And Ellen never understood why I spent so much time on something unrelated to school.

Ana looked touched as she took the notebook paper and carefully smoothed it out.

"Thank you."

"No problem," I said, and let out a breath I hadn't realized I'd been holding.

Ana walked me out to the porch. We decided she'd tutor me during lunch. As I was leaving, I said, "Did you ever join any of those clubs?"

"No," Ana said quickly. "I decided I didn't want to. See you tomorrow." Then she said good-bye and shut the door.

As I walked home, I looked up at the stars. They looked like thousands of diamonds twinkling against black velvet. I wondered why Ana had decided not to join any clubs. She had seemed so excited—like middle-school life held endless opportunities for her. What made her change her mind?

Chapter 8

✳   ✳   ✳

Super Freaky Glasses Rule #7
If you want to catch someone in a lie using your glasses,
you'll have to do it in person.

ANA WAS A GREAT TUTOR. WE MET A FEW TIMES A WEEK, and she never made fun of my Spanish pronunciation. And she didn't think I was weird (or rude) when I told her that every time I said, *"Me llamo Callie,"* I imagined myself riding llamas. Instead Ana laughed and said she thought the English expression "easy as pie" was kind of dumb.

"I've made pies with my *abuelita*—my grandma," she said. "Believe me, it's not easy."

One Friday before a big test, I asked Ana if she could help me study. Ana said she was spending the weekend at her Aunt Rosa's, but she invited me over to spend the day with her there. Ana and Aunt Rosa, a kind woman who reminded me a lot of Ana, took turns quizzing me on Spanish verbs.

My pronunciation improved, and soon Señora Geck stopped cringing when I spoke in class, and I stopped worrying Mom was going to ground me over my Spanish grade. Which was a good thing. Because I had more important things to worry about.

I thought not going to the Fall Dance was a wise move. That way all the things I worried would happen, wouldn't. But I should've thought more about what would happen if I *didn't* go.

Which was this: Ellen went with Stacy, and they spent the evening hanging out with a group of girls from their history class. Ellen called her parents from the dance, and asked them if she could spend the night at Stacy's. According to Stacy, it was *way* fun. But she totally understood why I didn't want to go—and thought it was a good idea that I stayed home.

Riiiight.

As the days passed, I played detective. When I saw Ellen and Stacy wearing the same shade of nail polish on Monday, I figured that meant they hung out over the weekend. And when my super-sleuth skills spied Ellen not paying attention in math class (a first for Ellen) because she was scribbling a note—a note she never gave to me—I spied on her thoughts and realized she was passing notes with Stacy.

Ellen and Stacy joined the same clubs, even though I knew from spying on Stacy's thoughts she didn't care about any of them.

Another thing I found out from spying on Stacy's thoughts: She was always thinking about the girl with the dull blond hair and green rubber-band braces—Green Braces Girl, I called her. Once when Ellen, Stacy, and I were walking down the hall, we saw a bunch of girls laughing at another girl with a bad case of acne. I'd just been glad they weren't laughing at *me*. But when I looked over at Stacy, I saw, in the screen hovering next to her, an image of a group of kids laughing at Green Braces Girl in what looked like a school cafeteria. For the millionth time, I'd wondered who Green Braces Girl was, and why Stacy thought about her all the time.

"What's this?" I held a folded up piece of paper Ana gave me. We were standing in my kitchen. Class had dismissed early for a minimum day, and Ana agreed to help me with an extra-credit project Señora Geck assigned. After cooking an authentic Mexican dish, I needed to write a one-page report (in English, thankfully) about what I learned.

I opened the paper and scanned the page. It was a rec-ipe. "What's mole sauce?" I said, picturing a furry little creature swimming in red sauce.

Ana laughed. "It's not 'mole' sauce. It's 'moe-*lay*' sauce. It's a traditional Mexican dish. We can make it for your project."

"You're kidding me. Can't we just buy it in a can or jar or something?" I didn't want to sound ungrateful, but there were, like, fifteen ingredients on the list. Truth-fully, when I agreed to cook something for extra credit, I'd envisioned myself browning ground beef, tossing in some shredded cheese, dumping canned salsa over the whole thing, and wrapping it all up in a tortilla. *Voila!* Tacos a la Callie!

But—call me a genius—I guessed that wasn't how Ana's family did it in Mexico.

"This is my *abuelita*'s famous recipe. She even won a contest once," Ana said.

"Okay." I looked around the kitchen. No way did we have half the ingredients on the list. I didn't even know what some of them were. I'd never heard of a guajillo chile before. And really, mixing a chile and a stick of cinnamon together sounded kind of nasty.

"I don't think I have enough money for all this." Mom

had given me some money so we could walk to the grocery store, but I was pretty sure I'd need more.

Ana looked at the list again. "We have most of the spices at home." She headed for the door. "I'll get them and be right back."

After Ana left I ransacked my kitchen, but the only ingredients I found were limp-looking sticks of celery and snack packs of raisins.

Ana returned with a brown paper bag full of spices, cans of chicken broth, onions, and what I thought at first was a small onion but turned out to be a head of garlic.

I grabbed a tote bag, dropped my glasses and money inside and headed for the door, but Ana stopped me.

"We will wait for Ellen, yes?"

I'd never made plans to hang out with someone other than Ellen before. I'd felt a little strange. Guilty, almost. So I invited Ellen over too. Ellen said she had a few club meetings after school, but she'd come over as soon as she could.

"Ellen's coming later," I said, and opened the door.

Ana passed the grocery store Mom and I usually shopped at and headed toward the Mexican market next door. I'd seen the market a million times before, but had never been inside. So I felt weird following behind Ana, like I was an imposter or something.

Ana passed the meat counter and hanging packages of dried peppers and went straight for the produce section. She picked through a bin of fresh peppers: plucking, weighing, and squeezing until she found just the right ones. While Ana shopped, I glanced around and saw a whole section of yummy-looking pastries. Some of them were even decorated with a thick stripe of green, white, and red frosting to look like the Mexican flag.

Once we selected our items, Ana handed me the basket and pointed to the cashier. "I want you to say, 'I want to buy these, please' in Spanish."

"No way. I can barely say my own name in Spanish."

"It is easy. You only say, *'Quiero comprar estos, por favor.'*"

"Only." I rolled my eyes. "Right."

Ana repeated the phrase a few times and then I went up to the counter. I probably butchered every word, but the cashier nodded and smiled as she rang up the items.

Outside, Ana stopped at a newspaper dispenser. She wanted to buy a paper she said Mr. Garcia liked to read. While she dug around in her pockets for quarters, I waited. The doors to the grocery store slid open, spitting out Raven and one of her Goth friends. Both held candy bars and canned sodas. I thought I heard her friend mutter "conformists," in a disgusted tone of voice when she saw Ana and me.

Which I thought was really funny. Raven and her friend were dressed so alike (down to their matching dog collars) they could have been twins.

Raven and her friend whispered and pointed at us while Ana, oblivious, fed her change into the newspaper dispenser. If Raven could spy on me, I figured I could spy on her. So I took my glasses from my tote bag and slipped them on.

The air shimmered and the blue screen appeared by Raven, and her thoughts scrolled across: *Is that how they dress in Mexico? She thinks she's so hot she can dress any way she wants and get away with it?*

Raven raised her voice. "Can her clothes be any tackier?"

"Can your attitude be any snottier?" I shot back.

I took my glasses off and bit back a smile. After weeks of seeing people's thoughts, and having to keep quiet, it felt *really* good to finally say something back.

"Sensitive, much?" Raven said. "I was just joking. You don't have to take everything so personally. Besides, I wasn't talking about *you*, Four Eyes."

Seeing Cinderella ★ 89

Raven and her Goth friend sauntered away, sipping sodas and laughing as they left.

Ana finished tucking the newspaper into a grocery bag and stood up. "What did she say? I didn't hear."

"We were just talking about . . . how neither of us likes drama."

That answer seemed to satisfy Ana, and I was glad. How could I explain Raven was making fun of the way Ana dressed? Personally, I didn't think Raven should talk, since she couldn't be bothered to wear something non-black. But Raven's clothes fit her, and most of Ana's didn't. Ana seemed to have only a handful of outfits: jeans that were too short, colorful stretch pants, a few T-shirts, skirts that were way too long, and the pair of too-short overalls she wore today.

I figured Ana's family in Mexico was probably poor, especially since her dad was sick.

So what was I supposed to do? Tell Ana to tell her uncle she needed trendier clothes?

On the walk back home, Ana asked me why I didn't like drama.

"I don't know," I said. "Sometimes I feel like there's this all-seeing eye just waiting for me to screw up."

"You mean God?"

"No. I mean the entire student body of Pacificview. They're not as nice as God."

"Maybe," Ana said. "But I think you are too scared sometimes. Like with the paint crew last week."

Last week, the paint crew started working on set pieces, beginning with the pumpkin patch near Cinderella's cottage. Most students dove right in with the orange paint. Their pumpkins looked like ginormous tangerines. I hung back, mixing the orange and white and brown paints until I had a perfect pumpkin shade. Ana watched me, and after a few minutes she whispered, "Show the others." But I kept quiet, until Gretchen Baxter glanced over and said, "Hey everyone, look at Callie." Since then, the crew regularly asked me how to mix colors, fix splatters, and paint shadows—all the things I learned from my dad.

"Maybe you're right," I said finally.

Back home, I took orders from Ana. I chopped onions until my eyes stung, and diced garlic until my hands reeked. Ana was amazing. She fried sesame seeds, toasted almonds, crushed tomatoes with her bare hands, and melted chocolate. After a while we had a large pot of red bubbly sauce that smelled sharp and sweet at the same time. Maybe I'd been wrong about peppers and cinnamon sticks not belonging together. Maybe in the right environment, they were just what the other one needed.

Ana told me her uncle really appreciated Mexican home cooking. I asked if she ever cooked like this for the Garcias.

Ana shrugged. "Tío says the more I cook and save money on food, the more money he can send to my parents."

That sounded weird to me. Mom was always complaining about money lately. But that didn't mean I got stuck cooking every night.

But when I said that to Ana, she replied, "I think maybe my family is different from yours. My list is a little longer." Then she pointed to the Post-it note of chores my mother had left for me by the phone.

"Oh, okay." I guessed Ana was right—her family *was* different from mine. There was a lot about her, and her culture, that I didn't understand. So I decided to change the subject.

"I wonder where Ellen is?" I asked, looking at the clock above the kitchen table. Her club meetings had to have ended by now.

Ana glanced up at the clock too, and her eyes widened. "Four fifty?" Quickly, she wiped her hands off on a towel. "I have to go."

"Go? You're not eating with us? You've done most of the work."

"I was supposed to make dinner for everyone tonight."

Ana headed for the door and I called, "Wait. What if we split the *mole* sauce? It's almost done anyway, and there's a ton. You take half and I'll take half."

Ana paused, and I could see relief in her eyes. "Okay. *Gracias*, thank you."

As soon as I put a lid on Ana's half of the sauce she scooped up the plastic container, calling *"Gracias"* again over her shoulder and streaking out the kitchen door.

After Ana left I decided to call Ellen and find out why she'd never shown up. A giggling voice picked up on the other line.

"Hello?" It was Ellen.

"Hey, it's me. When are you coming over?"

"Um . . ." There were hushed whispers on the other line, and a bubbling laugh I was sure belonged to Stacy.

"For dinner, remember? My extra-credit project?"

"Oh, Callie, I'm so totally sorry." Ellen's voice sounded sugary sweet. "When I got home, Tara was here. She flew home a few days early for the weekend. She said we could go with her to the mall. We thought it would be fun."

"Who is we?" I asked, but I was pretty sure I knew.

"Me and Tara," Ellen said quickly. "We."

Deciding to perform an experiment, I reached for my tote bag and slipped on my glasses. I held the phone out in front of me and asked in a loud, clear voice, "So you can't come over tonight because you and Tara are hanging out? Just the two of you?"

I stared at the receiver as Ellen hesitated. But no screen appeared when she said, "Yeah, that's right. Just Tara and me."

We hung up then, and I took my glasses off. I figured you had to actually be looking at a person to read their thoughts.

Or catch them in a lie.

Chapter 9

✷ ✷ ✷

Super Freaky Glasses Rule #8
*When it comes to best friends, all's fair in love
and middle school.*

ELLEN HAD LIED TO ME ON THE PHONE, I WAS SURE OF IT.
So I decided to spy on her thoughts the next morning, and find out for certain. But Ellen was late to first period. And trying to read her thoughts during class proved useless, because she was actually paying attention to Mrs. Faber.

"Are we boring you, Miss Anderson?" Mrs. Faber asked when she caught me staring at Ellen.

"No," I lied. "Not at all."

"Good." Mrs. Faber pointed to an equation on the whiteboard. "Then maybe you could tell me the answer to the problem the rest of us have been working on for the last five minutes?"

"Sure," I said, staring at the number inside the screen hovering by Mrs. Faber's head. "The answer is five and three-fourths."

"Correct." Mrs. Faber frowned, and the image inside the screen changed: *How did she know that? I know she wasn't paying attention.*

The bell rang then, and Ellen shot out of her seat, calling over her shoulder that she had another club meeting during lunch.

"Ellen, wait!" I yelled, as she hurried out the door, but she didn't hear me. By the time I caught up, Ellen was rummaging through her locker.

"Hey, how's it going?" I said.

"Not great." Ellen stuffed a textbook into her backpack. "I've got a history test next period I didn't study for." The screen appeared by Ellen. Inside was an image of Ellen and Stacy in Ellen's room. Stacy watched while Ellen strummed a guitar. Which confused me—I didn't think Ellen owned a guitar.

I felt sick to my stomach then and looked away from the screen. "Is . . . is there a reason why you didn't study for it?" I asked softly.

Ellen shut her locker and faced me. "Okay, look—Stacy spent the night last night. Okay? That's why I couldn't come over. Her dad was going out of town on a business trip and her mother decided to go. So they needed a place for Stacy to stay for a couple of nights. Stacy came over and brought her dad's old guitar. We started messing around with it and lost track of time. Okay?"

"Why didn't you just tell me this last night?" I asked.

"Because I know how much you hate Stacy."

"You didn't have to lie to me. And I don't hate Stacy."

"Well you act like you can't stand her, and I didn't want you getting all mad and making a big deal about it."

"I'm not making a big deal about it!"

"Yes, you are." Ellen crossed her arms, and we stared at each other as the warning bell rang.

I looked away first. "I'm sorry."

"It's okay," Ellen said quietly. Then she hefted her backpack over her shoulder. "Look—I don't want to be late to class. I'll see you in drama, okay?"

"Okay. Sorry," I said again.

As I watched Ellen sweep through the crowd, I wondered why I was the one who apologized when Ellen was the one who lied.

★ ★ ★

When I walked into drama class later that day, Ellen and Stacy whispered and giggled in the corner. Their fair heads were bent together, like the sun and moon were hugging each other. Watching them, I felt like Pluto. All cold and icy and distant.

As I neared them, I reminded myself to be nice and not to make a big deal about anything.

"What's so funny?" I asked in a cheery voice.

Ellen jumped like she'd been caught cheating on a test. "Nothing," she said, and Stacy nodded.

"Oh. I thought I heard you guys laughing?"

"You must be hearing things," Stacy said. "We were practicing our lines." She recited a line as the Wicked Stepmother.

"Oh, okay. Have fun then," I said, walking away and sinking into a chair next to Ana.

"Did your mom like the *mole* sauce?" Ana asked.

"Yeah," I said, not taking my eyes off Ellen and Stacy. "That's all we ate though, because I forgot to put the chicken in the oven."

Ana laughed and went back to her script.

The bell rang, and Mr. Angelo announced he was assigning partners to run lines. I tried to catch Ellen's eye, but she just listened to Stacy, who pointed at a poster on the wall advertising Pacificview Middle School's annual Halloween carnival.

Fine, be that way, I thought at Ellen, yanking my glasses from my backpack and slipping them on. She could ignore me all she wanted, but she couldn't hide from my super freaky magic glasses. Holding my script in front of me and pretending to study, I spied on Ellen and Stacy's thoughts.

Stacy: *The Halloween carnival sounds fun. I bet there'll be lots of boys.*

Ellen: *Callie and I hang out every Halloween. It's tradition.*

Stacy: *Why can't Ellen just tell Callie she doesn't want to do another boring sleepover?*

Ellen: *Maybe I could tell Callie I can't make it—and then meet Stacy at the carnival.*

I slumped in my seat. My eyes felt hot with tears and my throat felt thick. I wanted to cry and yell at Ellen—but I knew I couldn't. How could you argue with your best friend, when she never told you her true thoughts? When the only reason you know what she really thinks is because you're spying on her?

Before Ellen told me she "couldn't make it" on Halloween, I jumped up and marched over to them.

"Hey, I've got a great idea," I said.

"You do?" Stacy sounded skeptical. And so were her

thoughts: *What, like watching a bunch of cheesy horror movies? I swear, Callie likes the most boring things.*

I paused. Because last year after trick-or-treating, Ellen and I *had* watched a bunch of cheesy horror movies—and laughed ourselves silly. Which meant Ellen told her what we did last year. Did Ellen think that was boring now?

"Well, what's your wonderfully great idea?" Stacy prompted.

Since smacking Stacy right then would probably make Ellen mad (and get me suspended), I pointed to the poster instead.

"What if we went to the carnival instead of having a sleepover? We could get a big group of people together." I turned to Stacy. "You could come with us, if you want to."

Ellen stared at me, her thoughts slowly scrolling across the blue screen hovering next to her: *I wonder if it would be more fun to just go with Stacy.*

I felt something deflate inside me then, and I was about to say that maybe it wasn't such a good idea, after all.

But then Ellen shook her head slightly. *Stop it! Callie's your best friend. What kind of a person doesn't want to go to the carnival with her best friend? Besides, we had so much fun last year.*

"Sounds good," Ellen said. "Can we meet at your house like last year?"

"Sure," I said, smiling back at Ellen and holding out my pinkie. "It's tradition, isn't it?"

"I'll go," Stacy said, smiling widely as Ellen and I crossed pinkies. But her thoughts were not happy at all: *Why does Callie have to ruin everything?*

"Great," I said, floating off as Mr. Angelo called my name. From his thoughts, I knew he was about to pair me up with Scott Fowler.

Right then, I *loved* my glasses.

"Your beauty is exquisite. You're captivating. You're . . . you're . . ."

I leaned farther toward Scott. He was so close I could see the flecks of gold in his brown eyes. My heart raced and I was having trouble breathing. "Really? Tell me more."

"Your beauty is like . . . like—oh forget it!" Scott flung his script across the multipurpose room. "This Cinderella stuff is a bunch of junk. Good thing we're just understudies. Know what I mean? At least we don't have to really know any of it. Not like them." Scott pointed over to Charlie and Ellen, who also ran lines together.

Students sat scattered throughout the multipurpose room in groups of two. Mr. Angelo stood behind Charlie and Ellen; all three of them looked irritated.

"Come on, you two," Mr. Angelo said, "The Prince and Cinderella are supposed to fall madly in love at first sight."

"I *told* Charlie we should've signed up for wood shop instead of drama," Scott muttered.

I stared at Scott in a daze. I'd never been so close to him before. If I shut out the rest of the class I could imagine we really were at a ball. That we really were—

"Hello? Anybody home?" Scott waved a hand in front of my face.

I snapped back to attention, jerking my head back against the folding chair behind me.

"Ouch!" I rubbed my head.

"You don't talk much, do you?" Scott asked.

"W-well," I began, but stopped. I never actually talked to Scott last year. I just sat behind him—two desks away, to be exact—admiring his poems. Every response that came to me seemed dorky, and I didn't want Scott to think I was a weirdo.

I took my glasses out of my backpack and slipped them on. Then I turned back to Scott. But he'd given up trying to talk to me, and was glancing around the room, looking bored.

"Come on, people," Mr. Angelo hollered to the class.

"Use this time to get to know your character. Learn your character. Become your character."

The air around Scott shimmered and the screen appeared next to him: *Mr. Angelo needs to get a grip. He takes this drama stuff way too seriously. Why does Charlie like him so much?*

Then his thoughts turned to the weekend: *Maybe Charlie and I could see a movie this Saturday.*

"S-so," I began, but stopped again. I almost asked him if he was going to the movies this weekend, but I thought he might get suspicious. Or worse, he might think I wanted to ask him out.

But the screen hovering next to him showed me he thought something else: *Dude, Callie is* weird. *Has she got a speech problem or something?*

I didn't know if I should've felt hurt that he thought I was weird, or happy that he now knew my name was Callie instead of Carrie. I went with happy. And instead of asking him about his weekend plans, I decided to talk about mine.

"Stacy, Ellen, and I are going to the Halloween carnival this weekend," I said. "Think you'll go?"

"Yeah, I think Charlie and I are hanging out," Scott said. His next thought sent my heart fluttering: *Maybe I should ask them to go with us. She's cute.*

I swear, I almost fainted right then. Scott Fowler

thought I was cute! Me—Polka Dot—with the frizzy hair and freckly face! I bit the inside of my cheek, to keep from saying yes before he actually asked. But then Mr. Angelo had to go and ruin the moment.

"You're not practicing your lines," he said, handing Scott back his script. "Understudies are quite important, you know. You must be prepared to carry on the show at a moment's notice if one of the leads becomes sick or is otherwise unable to perform."

"Whatever," Scott said. "Charlie never gets sick."

"Yeah, neither does Ellen," I said. *So could you please leave,* I added silently. *I'm about to get asked out on my first sort-of date!*

But the spell was broken.

"I guess we'd better work on this," Scott said, looking at his script. *I hate drama,* he was thinking.

So do I, I thought back at Scott as I glared at Mr. Angelo's retreating figure. *Believe me, so do I.*

Chapter 10

✵ ✵ ✵

Super Freaky Glasses Rule #9
*It's easier to dislike someone when you don't
have to read their thoughts.*

"CALLIE, GET THE DOOR!" MOM'S VOICE SCREECHED UP
the stairs.

I looked in the mirror, and stuck my tongue out
at my goofy reflection. Last year, Ellen insisted we buy
matching yellow rag-doll costumes. It cost me a month's
allowance, but Ellen said it was cute, and that we could
wear them the next year. But we forgot one small thing:
growth spurts.

Now the costume's skirt hung a couple inches above
my knees; so I had pulled a pair of black stretch pants
on underneath—making me look like a freckly honeybee.

Since Ellen was a few inches taller than me, I wondered if she would think the skirt was too short also.

I shouldn't have worried.

"Happy Hallowee—" I broke off as I opened the front door and saw Ellen and Stacy—dressed identically as a trendy Little Red Riding Hood, complete with swishy red-and-white skirts, clunky red shoes, and red choker necklaces.

"That's a way cute costume," Stacy said, stepping inside and brushing past me. "I had one just like it when I was in third grade."

"Thanks," I said, staring hard at Ellen. "Ellen and I bought it last year."

Ellen wore an apologetic expression on her face as she stepped inside. She should be sorry. True, we never actually *said* we were wearing our rag-doll costumes tonight—but that had been the whole point when we bought them last year.

So while I looked six years old, Ellen and Stacy looked like middle-school models. Maybe I stunk at algebra, but I could still do the math: If Ellen and Stacy wore identical costumes, then they planned it—without including me. I probably wouldn't have dressed up as Little Red Riding Hood (my hair and freckles were red enough), but it would've been nice if they'd asked.

I moved to shut the door when a rough voice said, "Wait."

I looked in disbelief at Raven, who skulked in wearing her usual black shirt, black jeans, and dog collar.

"Dig your costume," Raven said, smirking.

"Hello, girls," Mom said, walking into the hallway. "Oh you both look so lovely," she said to Ellen and Stacy. "And what are you supposed to be?" she turned to Raven.

Raven looked confused. "What do you mean?"

"Your costume. Are you a witch?"

"I'm not wearing a costume. These are my normal clothes," Raven said.

"Oh, of course. My mistake," Mom said, and scurried away.

"Where's your room?" Stacy asked. "I need to fix my makeup."

"Upstairs, second one on the right."

Stacy and Raven filed up the stairs. Ellen started to follow until I grabbed her arm.

"What is Raven doing here?" I whispered.

Ellen shrugged. "Raven heard Stacy and me talking in science class, and Stacy invited her. She's really not that bad. She's a good lab partner, actually."

"Yeah, and I'll bet Raven lets you do most of the work."

"So what?" Ellen said. "It wouldn't be any different if *you* were my lab partner."

I closed my mouth. She had me there.

"And anyway," Ellen continued, "you're the one who said we should get a group of people together. I didn't think you'd mind—I don't think Raven has very many friends." Ellen started walking upstairs. "Where's Ana?"

"She's not here yet," I said, following behind Ellen.

Inside my room Stacy lounged on a throw pillow. "Cool wall," she said, leaning her head against my daisy mural.

"Yeah," Raven said, slumping at my desk chair. "It's really shiny and happy."

I ignored Raven. "Thanks, my dad and I painted it."

"You painted it yourself?" Stacy said, sounding awed. "Hey—you know what would be cool? Painting murals on all the other walls. That way, no matter where you sat it would feel like you were outside." Stacy looked at me. "I could help you paint, if you wanted."

"Um, I'll think about it," I said.

With one last look at the mural, Stacy popped up, opened her ginormous purse, and tipped it over, unleashing an ocean of makeup on my dresser.

Stacy and Ellen started primping in front of my

dresser mirror like it was the prom, instead of just Pacific-view's Halloween carnival. Stacy picked through the pile of makeup and pulled out a brown tube she offered my way. "I've got a concealer stick," she said. "You know, in case you want to cover up your freckles."

"Not enough makeup in the world for that," I heard Raven mutter under her breath.

"No thanks," I said to Stacy. My mom didn't allow me to wear makeup yet. And even if she did, my skin was so oily the concealer would end up, well, *concealed* in puddles of grease anyway.

I continued to watch them, feeling like I was a guest in my own room. So I did what I was starting to do every time I felt nervous: I put my glasses on.

The air waved and shimmered and blue screens launched up by Stacy, Ellen, and Raven.

Raven stared at Stacy and Ellen, looking just as uncomfortable as I felt. Inside the screen hovering by her, white words scrolled across a blue screen: *Maybe coming here was a mistake. Maybe I should've stayed home with Mom and her loser boyfriend after all.*

The screen next to Stacy showed a picture of Green Braces Girl sitting alone on a couch with a bowlful of candy.

Stacy frowned at her reflection, wiped off her lipstick, and grabbed a different color tube. When she caught me looking at her, her thoughts changed: *What is she looking at? She can be so judgmental sometimes.*

I looked away. Was I judgmental? From reading people's thoughts I already knew sometimes they thought I was stuck-up because I didn't talk a lot. I was trying to change that, though. Hadn't it been my idea to get everyone together tonight in the first place?

But judgmental? Was that me? I felt mad, and ashamed, and confused, all at the same time. I wasn't sure what Stacy meant, and I almost wanted to tell her I was sorry.

But then I shook myself. Stacy was trying to steal my best friend. I wasn't apologizing to *her* for anything.

"What time is Ana coming?" Ellen asked.

"*She's* coming?" Raven asked. "Why?"

"Callie invited her," Ellen said. "Ana's her Spanish tutor."

I should have said something then. Something about how Ana was my friend, not just my tutor. But Raven's searing glare sealed my mouth shut.

"Whatever," Raven said, picking up a compact and beginning to apply white powder to her already chalky skin. "She can't even speak English right."

I flinched, figuring she meant Ana's accent. Raven scowled at her reflection in the mirror. In the screen hovering next to her, her thoughts were just as nasty as her words. Except she wasn't thinking about Ana, she was thinking about herself: *But Ana's not even American and she reads better than you, little miss reads-at-a-fourth-grade-level. What kind of an idiot are you? Why can't you see words like normal people instead of jumbling them all up?*

Raven Maggert was the last person I wanted to feel sorry for—but I did anyway. Words never jumbled up on me, and I still struggled in school. From spying on Raven's thoughts I knew she stressed out whenever we had to read aloud in history, English, or drama class. I guess now I knew why.

"It's been really helpful, having a tutor," I said carefully.

"People who need tutors are losers," Raven said.

Raven went back to powdering herself into a ghost. Ellen stared defiantly in the mirror while she fluffed her bangs, and I read the screen hovering next to her, showing me her thoughts: *I'm tired of being good little Ellen all the time. No matter how much or how well I do, Tara always does better. I've had it. Mom can refuse to buy me a guitar—but she's still going to see a different Ellen this year. She can just deal with the changes.*

"What changes?" I asked, and then froze. I'd said it out loud. Not good. *So* not good.

But I don't think Ellen even realized I'd read her thoughts. She just stared at me in the mirror as different images flashed on the screen hovering near her. Ellen, at what I thought was a club meeting, looking bored. Ellen glancing over at a boy in the cafeteria, then blushing when he smiled at her. Ellen laughing with Stacy while they played around with the guitar. The screen changed again, and one sentence scrolled across: *Callie wouldn't understand.*

Callie wouldn't understand. I was so sick of reading about how "Callie wouldn't understand."

"Why are you wearing those?" Ellen asked suddenly, turning around and facing me.

"Wearing what?" I looked down at my costume.

"Your glasses. You told me you only need them for reading, but you wear them all the time."

"Um . . ." I glanced around my room, hoping to find a good excuse. Because telling Ellen the truth was so *not* an option.

"I thought—I thought they'd go well with my costume."

"It definitely adds to the loser factor," Raven said.

"Well it looks ridiculous." Ellen's thoughts told me she wasn't buying it. *She's lying. I always know when Callie's lying.*

"Give them to me." Ellen held out her hand.

I didn't want to *give* Ellen the glasses. I wanted to *throw* them at her. At the demanding hands she held out, hands that just assumed I'd obey her. And I wanted to yell—yell at all of them—and tell them they weren't allowed to boss me around, or say mean things about me, my costume, or my freckles. Not in my own room. Maybe in the hallways of Pacificview I was just the frizzy-haired girl with freckles and ugly glasses. But in my room, I was the queen. And no one was allowed to be mean to me.

But if I said any of that, Ellen would tell me I was being ridiculous, Raven would say I was too sensitive, and Stacy would giggle and secretly wonder if Ellen and I were about to break up as best friends. So I did what everyone in the room expected me to do: I politely handed the glasses to Ellen.

And watched in horror as she stuck them on her face.

Think nothing but nice thoughts, I commanded myself frantically, squeezing my eyes shut. Don't think about how much you don't like Stacy, how you think Raven is nasty, or most of all, how mad you get at Ellen. Just think nice, happy thoughts. And you'd better start thinking of a darn good apology: *I'm so sorry I've been spying on you guys. Really, I didn't mean to do it. Okay, well I guess I did. But I didn't do it that often. Only when I was mad, or nervous, or frustrated. Which has been a lot this year.*

I am so dead, I thought as Ellen continued to stare at me.

After what seemed like forever, Ellen took them off and said, "Your eyesight stinks, Callie. I can't see anything in these!"

Stacy giggled, and I breathed a sigh of relief as I took my glasses back.

"You guys finish getting ready. I'm going next door to get Ana." I hoped they didn't hear my voice shake as I backed out the door.

That was close.

Chapter 11

✲ ✲ ✲

Super Freaky Glasses Rule #10

Never leave home without your glasses
(and a pack of Red Hots).
You never know when they might come in handy.

ANGRY VOICES SPURTED FROM AN OPEN WINDOW AS I walked up the porch to Ana's house. The voices fell silent when I knocked, and I heard footsteps padding toward the front door. I hoped Ana would answer so I wouldn't have to talk to her uncle. I wasn't disappointed.

"*Hola.*" Ana stepped out onto the porch. Behind her, I saw Mr. Garcia lurking in the entryway, staring at us. I wondered what they had been arguing about.

"Ready to go?" I asked, although clearly Ana wasn't ready. Instead of the nurse's costume she said she had, Ana was dressed in her too-small overalls. I almost asked if she'd changed her mind and decided to go as a farmer, but didn't.

"I cannot go. I am sick," Ana said.

"Oh. Okay." I frowned, and not just because I felt disappointed, but because I had this strange feeling Ana was lying. She looked tired, so maybe she really was sick. But something about the way she held on to the door—like she couldn't wait to close it—made me feel like she was lying. If Ana had gotten in trouble with her uncle, she could've just told me.

Then again, she probably couldn't, I realized as I looked over her shoulder at Mr. Garcia. Not with him spying on us. I wished I could've put my glasses on and found out the truth. But after the close call with Ellen, I'd left them at home.

"See you at school." Ana sounded like Mr. Angelo when he dismissed us from class.

Ana stepped back inside her house. Something made me stick out my foot, catching the door before it closed.

"What are your symptoms?" I asked.

"Symptoms? I do not know this word."

"Symptoms, you know—coughing, sneezing." I faked a sneeze.

"Oh. I feel cold. And my head hurts."

"So you have a headache?"

"Yes. I have a headache. Good-bye, Callie." I moved my foot, and Ana firmly shut the door.

I stared at the door, wishing I'd brought my glasses. Wishing I could've tried to read Ana's thoughts, even if most of them were in Spanish.

Because I knew Ana was lying to me. What I didn't know was why.

The scent of popcorn, hot dogs, and cotton candy wafted down the street and met us as we walked to Pacificview. Raven and I trudged behind Ellen and Stacy. Cars honked as they raced by us.

I patted my costume, relaxing when I felt my glasses. After leaving Ana's house, I decided I wanted them with me at the Carnival. So I tucked them into the pocket underneath my apron. I just felt . . . *safer* having them with me.

Loud music and shouts and the roar of a roller coaster greeted us as we neared Pacificview Middle School. Dusk had deepened and a Ferris wheel rose up over the tops of Pacificview's buildings into a pink-and-purple streaked sky.

"What do you guys want to do first?" Stacy asked when we arrived.

"I'm hungry," Raven said.

I looked over to the snack stands and saw Scott and Charlie eating hot dogs. "I'm hungry too," I said quickly.

While we ordered sodas, french fries, and a bucket of popcorn, I kept my eye on Scott. If he'd almost asked me to go to the carnival, then he'd come over as soon as he noticed me.

I was right.

"Ahoy thar, me ladies, be this the isle of sustenance? We've come in search of refreshments for our weary souls." Charlie wore a pirate costume, complete with an eye patch, a gold earring, and a stuffed parrot sitting on his shoulder. Scott stood next to him, looking totally cute dressed in a martial arts costume.

Raven rolled her eyes, but Ellen and Stacy giggled.

Charlie grabbed a french fry off my plate, which I could tell Ellen thought was rude, but I didn't care. Scott Fowler was standing four feet away from me!

"Aye, french fries, just what my aching soul is craving," Charlie said, stealing another fry.

"May your soul be refreshed." I pushed my plate toward him. Who could eat? When Scott Fowler was standing. Four. Feet. Away. From. Me!

Everyone laughed while Charlie pretended to feed his stuffed parrot a few fries.

"Where are you guys headed after this?" I asked Scott.

"Over to the Monster's Mirror Maze," Charlie answered.

"Want to join us?" Scott asked.

Hmmm, let me think about that for one—

"Okay," Ellen and Stacy chorused, before I could say anything.

At the maze, Ellen suggested we team up in partners and have a race. Scott and Charlie took off, and Ellen said, "Who wants to be my partner?"

"I do!" Stacy and I both said.

Ellen looked from me to Stacy, her head swiveling like she was watching a tennis match. Then she said, "I'll be partners with Raven." Ellen ran into the maze, followed by a not-very-excited-looking Raven.

"Come on, Stacy. Let's go," I said impatiently. Maybe I could catch up to Charlie and Scott. Maybe then Scott and I could talk, and maybe then, well, who knew?

But Stacy seemed entranced by the mirrors, and kept lagging behind. Finally I gave up trying to hurry her and stared at the mirrors too.

In one mirror my ears looked twice the size of my head, reminding me of a pair of oversize cymbals. In another mirror, Stacy's body plumped out while her head looked like a shrunken raisin. Stacy stopped and studied herself, seeming to forget I was there.

"Come on," I said. "Everyone else is probably finished by now."

Stacy didn't hear me. She stood still, looking grimly at her own reflection.

"Stacy, let's go. Stacy?"

Still no answer. Stacy stared at herself with this funny look on her face. And—I couldn't help it—I took out my glasses to spy on her thoughts.

A few girls came streaming through the maze, giggling just as I slipped on my glasses.

They're laughing at me, Stacy's thoughts scrolled across the blue screen hovering next to her. *Some things never change. No matter how hard you try.*

"They weren't—" I began, but broke off quickly. I didn't want Stacy getting suspicious about the glasses, like Ellen earlier.

It didn't matter. Stacy hadn't heard me.

No matter what, I'll always be that *girl.*

What girl? I wanted to ask, but knew I couldn't. It occurred to me then I knew very little about Stacy. I knew she'd moved to California from Oregon over the summer, that she was boy crazy, and that she was out to steal my best friend. But I didn't know anything else. I'd never bothered to ask.

"So what—" I began, but Stacy took off, seeming to instinctively know her way out of the maze.

"We won!" Ellen raised her fist triumphantly when we came out of the maze.

But she didn't point to Raven—she pointed to Scott.

"I lost Raven in the maze," Ellen was saying. "And Scott lost Charlie, so we teamed up. And we won!" Ellen and Scott high-fived.

Okay, so any interest I might have felt in Stacy's life just totally flatlined, like one of those heart monitors on TV. *I* could've been the one who found Scott in the maze, but nooooooo, Stacy the slowpoke had to go and ruin it.

After that, Ellen suggested we head over to the games section.

While Scott tossed footballs through a tire, I pulled a pack of Red Hots from my apron pocket and started crunching on them. I must have been standing really close to Scott, because when he pulled back his arm he knocked into me, sending my Red Hots skittering into the grass.

Scott turned back, looking annoyed. When he saw the Red Hots though, he flashed his crooked smile. "Are those your favorite candy?"

"Aar, she sneakest them all the time in class," Charlie said, before I could answer. Then he turned to me and added, "It makes your tongue really red."

I blushed, and Scott turned back and lobbed the football. It sailed easily through the tire, earning him a stuffed teddy bear for his effort. And then he turned around and offered it to . . . me!

"Sorry about your Red Hots," he said.

"No problem," I replied, dazed. Scott Fowler had just won me a teddy bear.

Maybe this night wasn't totally ruined after all.

Chapter 12

✵ ✵ ✵

Super Freaky Glasses Rule #11
People guard their secrets well.
Your magic glasses can't change that.

"Calliope, wake up! It's eleven in the morning. It's late even for a Saturday." Mom pounded on the door.

"Umagettinup," I mumbled from under my bedspread. After a few more door pounds, Mom left, allowing me to resume my dreams. Most of them featured Scott reading his poems to me on a tropical beach before we rode off into the sunset on a unicorn.

Okay, maybe that was over the top. But Scott had won me a teddy bear—proof, I'd thought last night, that he was totally crushing on me. Until Stacy opened her big mouth.

"Hey, no fair," she had protested, after Scott handed me the bear. "We want one too."

Then Ellen got all royal and said, "Yes, kind Prince, and as your Cinderella I shall require the best bear in all the land."

Next thing I knew Scott had spent a few more dollars, and soon all the girls had their own bears except for Raven, who told everyone she thought teddy bears were stupid. Still though, Scott had given *me* the first bear he won. That had to mean something.

I picked up my teddy bear (who I'd already named Scotty), and hugged him once before depositing him back on my pillow. I rolled toward my nightstand and picked up my phone. I wanted to talk to Ellen about Scott—without Stacy hanging around.

"Martin residence," came a prim voice on the other line.

"Hi, Mrs. Martin. Is Ellen around?"

"Oh, hello, Callie." Mrs. Martin's voice warmed up. "It's been ages. How come I never see you anymore?"

"I don't know," I mumbled, but Mrs. Martin didn't hear.

"Ellen's not here. She's out with Stacy. I'll tell her you called, though."

"Oh, okay. Thanks, Mrs. Martin." My voice cracked as I said good-bye.

I hung up my phone, and flopped backward. My pillow made a poufing sound, and Scotty spilled to the ground. I stared up at the ceiling, thinking.

The day after the carnival Ellen decided to hang out with Stacy. Without me. I felt something shift then, like Stacy had just won a major victory.

"Best friends forever," I whispered, holding out my pinkie.

But Ellen wasn't there to meet me halfway. As I lowered my arm, I realized I didn't have another friend I could call.

The phone rang then, and I hoped, hoped, *hoped* it was Ellen, inviting me to join her and Stacy. Fast as a Wicked Stepsister finding an oversize glass slipper, I snatched up the phone.

"Ellen?"

"Not quite, Callie Cat," my dad said, laughing. "I guess you'll have to settle for your poor old man. Have you written any stories about me lately?"

"No, Dad," I said, hoping he didn't hear the disappointment in my voice. "But I promise to write a few before next weekend."

"Actually, that's why I called. I can't make it."

"What?" I said, my thoughts momentarily distracted

from Ellen and Stacy the Best-Friend Stealer. "But we haven't seen you in forever—you keep saying you're coming to see us, and then you always cancel. When are you coming home? And when are you and Mom going to make up?"

Out came all the questions I'd learned not to ask when Mom kicked Dad out. Because asking them seemed to hurt both my parents.

"Things take time, Callie Cat. And your mother . . . well, you know how your mother is."

I sighed. I did know.

"So, when *can* you come see us then, if you can't make it next weekend?" I hated it that when I said those words, in my head I heard them in Mom's voice.

"Not for some time, I'm afraid. Not for about six or seven weeks or so."

"What? Six weeks? Why?"

"I've got some things I need to take care of."

"What things?"

Dad paused, and I could hear him sigh on the other line. "Things you won't understand until you're older."

I always hated it when parents said stupid stuff like that. How did they know what their kids would or wouldn't understand? It seemed to me that half the time, kids were smarter than their parents. I wanted to use my glasses and find out what these "things" were that I was too young to understand, but I already knew from trying that on Ellen it was useless.

"Fine," I said, deciding not to argue. "Want to talk to Mom?"

"No." My dad now sounded eager to get off the phone. "I talked to her last night. Take care, Callie Cat. Love you lots."

"Love you lots, too."

I hung up the phone and hauled myself out of bed, my great mood when I first woke up now totally gone. I slipped on my glasses, grabbed my journal, and headed downstairs.

Ellen might've been unavailable, but I still wanted to talk to someone about Scott. So I went to my last resort: my mother.

Mom was in her office grading papers, her usual Saturday morning routine.

"Hi, Mom."

"Hello," she said, not looking up. A red pen flashed across the page she graded. "We went over and over this, and they still don't get it," she mumbled to herself. "Who was on the phone?" she asked a second later.

"Dad."

The air shimmered, and the screen appeared by Mom. Inside, in fierce red writing, were her thoughts about Dad. They were full of words I wasn't allowed to say. Mom looked up and glanced at my journal. The screen changed then and an image appeared of my dad holding a painting and talking excitedly to Mom while she spooned baby food into Sarah's mouth with one hand, and scrambled eggs with the other.

"Have you been writing in that thing again?" she asked.

"Uh, no," I said, and carefully set it down on a bookcase. Mom went back to grading papers and I said, "The carnival was fun last night."

"Oh?" Mom said it like she wanted to hear more, but when I looked back at the screen near her I knew her thoughts were drifting away from Dad, and from me, and back to where they usually were—her classroom. *Did I schedule the math test for Tuesday or Wednesday? Where is my planner?*

"Yeah," I said as Mom began rummaging through piles on her desk. "We ran into some boys from our drama class."

"Good. That's good, honey." But then she found her planner, and her to-do list, and her thoughts drifted even farther away: *Grade the spelling test, ask Callie to do her chores, call the bank, ask Callie to do her chores, clean the bathroom . . .*

"Yeah," I said, pushing on, "and I was wondering if—"

"Have you unloaded the dishwasher?" Mom looked up.

"What? No. I just got up, remember?"

Mom closed her eyes and rubbed her temples. *Maybe if I send Callie to the park with Sarah, I could get everything done. I might as well unload the dishes myself, anyway.*

"Look, I'm sorry about the dishes. I'll do them in a minute, but I was wondering—"

Mom leaned around me and hollered. "Sarah! Can you come in here?" Then she looked up at me and said, "I need you to—"

"Take Sarah to the park so you can get some work done. Okay, *fine.*" I stomped out the door, passing Sarah in the hallway. If Mom wondered how I'd known what she was thinking, she never asked. She was too busy telling Sarah to get dressed.

My favorite tree lives in the park by our house. Squished between a couple palms and a few other evergreens stood one tree that was actually changing colors. After I got Sarah settled on the swings I sat down on a bench and stared at my tree. I liked looking at the red and brown and gold leaves. It made my heart rise up with a warm, hopeful feeling. Kind of like Thanksgiving and Christmas and the last day of school all rolled together.

Then I thought about Ellen and Stacy and my heart plunged like a broken elevator. It never bothered me before that I didn't have a ton of friends. I had Ellen, and she was better than a hundred friends.

But what if one day we weren't friends anymore?

I opened my backpack and pulled out my *Cinderella* script and my journal. If I couldn't talk to someone, I'd do something even better. I'd write a story.

Cinderella and Her New Friend

One day Cinderella got tired of living with her Wicked Stepsisters, who always did things without her and never let her in on their inside jokes. So she decided to ditch her sorry-looking bed under the chimney and find another place to live.

She ran far into the forest and found an abandoned cottage in a meadow. She lived there happily all summer, but eventually she became lonely. She even missed the friendly mice from her stepmother's attic. Each day she'd stand outside her cottage and sing at the top of her voice-hoping someone would hear. Day after day she came and sang, and just when the meadow turned cold and brown and she was about to give up, another girl her age stepped into the clearing and began to sing the same song. They went inside and passed the winter together singing and telling stories.

When I finished, I closed my journal. And I saw Ana.

She didn't see me as she herded the Garcia boys into the park. Anthony and Miguel started throwing sand at each other.

"Anthony! Miguel! Stop it!" Ana said, followed by something in Spanish.

The boys ignored her, and then, in English, Ana threatened to tell Mr. Garcia they weren't behaving.

"Go ahead and tell him," Anthony said. Then he threw a fistful of sand, which barely missed Ana's face. "See what he'll do."

I expected Ana to yell at him or turn around and march them straight back home. That's what I would've done, anyway, if Sarah acted like that. But Ana just got this really sad look on her face and said something to them in Spanish, and they skittered off to the play structure.

"Hi, Ana," I said.

Ana jumped and turned around. She seemed a little embarrassed. "*Hola,*" she said, and sat down next to me.

"Feeling better?" I asked.

"Better?"

"Yeah. Are you still sick?"

"No," Ana said quickly, a look of realization setting in. "I'm feeling much better."

We were silent, and I turned to watch Miguel and Sarah, who were over by the trees throwing leaves at each other. I think we both knew Ana was lying about being sick.

But it looked like we were both going to just let it go.

"Did you have fun at the carnival last night?" Ana asked quietly.

"Yeah. We ran into Scott Fowler and Charlie Ferris."

"Scott. The boy with the ponytail, yes? The one you like?"

I turned to Ana. "How did you know I like him?" I hadn't ever talked to Ana about my crush on Scott. Actually, I hadn't talked to Ellen about him either, at least not this year. The time just never seemed right. (Translation: Stacy was always hanging around hogging Ellen and the conversation.)

"What is that expression Americans use?" Ana paused. Then she smiled, and made a show of rolling her eyes. "Duh."

"Is it that obvious?"

Ana put her thumb and pointer finger together. "*Un poquito*. A little bit." She leaned over and pointed at my script. "Are you practicing with Ellen today?"

"No. She's busy." I felt a stabbing sensation and wondered if right then Ellen was practicing her Cinderella lines with Stacy. A role she wouldn't even have if it weren't for me.

"Want to share secrets?" I asked.

When Ellen and I were younger, we made up a game called "Sharing Secrets." Ellen would tell me a secret, and then I would tell her one. The first time we played, we huddled under a sleeping bag with our flashlights. Ellen confessed she overheard her parents wondering why she only got a B on her science project, because Tara always got A's in science. I confessed that when I overheard my parents it was usually because they were shouting at each other.

After I explained the game to Ana and told her I would go first, I said, "I was supposed to be Cinderella." I told her how Mr. Angelo offered me the lead. How I'd turned it down and given it to Ellen instead, because I knew Ellen wanted it more—even though sometimes I thought Ellen wasn't the greatest actress. And anyway, I knew I would just screw things up if I was Cinderella.

After I finished, I expected Ana to tell me what a great friend I was, or something like that.

But she didn't. "I think you would be a good Cinderella. I hear you practice. I think you could do it."

"Oh," I said, surprised. "Yeah, maybe."

I looked over toward the kids. Miguel careened down the slide. Anthony grabbed low-hanging twigs from a tree—my tree—and snapped them off from the branch, while Sarah tried to catch a butterfly.

I looked back at Ana. "It's your turn."

"What?"

"It's your turn to share a secret."

Ana stared at me silently. "I know I'm lucky to live here," she began and paused. "My family is very lucky that Tío lets me live with him. But he said—" Ana cut herself off. "But there was something—"

Sarah's screams interrupted Ana. She flailed over to me, followed by Anthony, who, in my opinion, looked totally guilty.

"Callie! He threw sand in my face!" Sarah jabbed her finger at Anthony.

"Did not!"

"Did too!"

Ana began speaking to Anthony in Spanish, and I took

the opportunity to grab my glasses from my backpack and read Anthony's thoughts, which, thankfully, were all in English. He did throw sand in Sarah's face, and was feeling pretty pleased with himself about it. He planned to throw more sand at Sarah, and had some hidden in his pocket. He was actually hoping he'd get caught so Ana would make them all go home. That way he could finish the video game he'd been playing.

Miguel came up to Ana then, asking for a drink of water. While Ana answered him, I leaned over and whispered to Anthony, "You'd better empty out your pockets, because if you even think about throwing sand at my little sister again, I will make those precious little video games of yours go somewhere far, far away."

Anthony's eyes widened and he furiously pitched sand from his pockets.

"Good," I said. Then I turned to Sarah. "Problem solved. Now both of you go back to the swings and play nice." I shook my finger at Anthony. "And no more snapping twigs off the trees."

Anthony, Miguel, and Sarah all scampered away, and I turned back to Ana.

"Okay, go on," I said, taking off my glasses and polishing them with the hem of my T-shirt.

"What?" Ana looked confused.

"You didn't finish sharing your secret." I put my glasses back on.

Ana stared at me steadily. Finally she shrugged and said, "My secret is sometimes I don't like America."

There was more to it than that, I was sure of it. The air shimmered, and in the blue screen that appeared next to Ana, tons and tons of Spanish words scrolled across. But other than a few words like *casa* (house) and *familia* (family), I didn't understand any of it. A few English words were mixed in there, too, but not enough to make sense of anything.

I realized that Ana's secret, even though it hovered right before me, would stay a secret. Unless one day she decided to share it with me.

Chapter 13

✳ ✳ ✳

Super Freaky Glasses Rule #12
It's no use crying over spilled Red Hots.
Plus, boys are stupid.

EARLY MONDAY MORNING, I COULDN'T GET MY LOCKER open. A red piece of paper was jammed between the door and the frame. The tenth time I spun the combination dial, the door finally sprang open, sending a shower of textbooks and loose papers cascading to the ground.

"What's all this junk?"

Behind me stood Raven. She wore a scowl, and a new dog collar—this one silver with black spikes.

"I told you not to mess with my stuff."

"Sorry." I started grabbing books and tossing them into our locker. "Something was jammed in the door.

"What's this?" I picked up a thick red envelope, stuffed with something squarelike inside. I flipped it over and realized it was addressed to me.

"Is this from you?" I asked Raven as I tore open the envelope.

Raven gave me a look that told me to get real, and started cleaning up.

Inside the envelope was a box of Red Hots. A red Post-it was stuck to it with a short note that read:

Enjoy! Try not to spill these ones!

"Hey, Princess Four Eyes, could use a little help here," Raven said, picking trash up off the ground.

"So hire a maid and stop bugging me," I snapped, and read the note a second time. Then out loud a third time. Raven just grunted in response and grabbed a couple of books from our locker. Then she stalked into the crowded hallway, calling over her shoulder, "Tell your loser boyfriend to keep his lame love notes out of my locker."

"Boyfriend?"

I flipped the Post-it over, but the other side was blank.

I looked up, dumbfounded. Did I have a secret admirer?

✷ ✷ ✷

"It was from Scott, I know it," I said to Ana at lunch. *"Él es muy estúpido!"*

"I think you mean *atractivo*, not *estúpido*," Ana said, smiling. "You just said Scott is very stupid."

"Right, sorry. *Él es muy, muy, muy atractivo.* He is soooooo cute!"

Ana kept trying to tutor me in Spanish. But I had more important subjects to discuss: Scott, Scott, and—wait for it—Scott!

Those Red Hots came from Scott, I was sure of it. Which meant I finally had the proof I needed: Scott liked me back!

"I know it was from him," I said, tapping the box of Red Hots, which I'd reverently placed in the middle of our lunch table. "You should've seen the look on his face when he made me spill my Red Hots. Then he won me Scotty, my teddy bear."

"I don't know, Callie. There's something about him," Ana said.

"What do you mean?"

"I don't know how to say it," Ana paused. "I don't like his smile. And I think he knows you think he's cute."

"So what? I *do* think he's cute. Do you think I should ask him to the Sadie Hawkins dance?"

The Sadie Hawkins dance was scheduled for the same Saturday as the play, just a few hours later. I knew this only because I'd heard Stacy agonizing for weeks over who she should ask, while Ellen wondered if she could wear her Cinderella costume to the dance. I hadn't paid much attention because I hadn't planned on going. But that was about to change. Because of the note and the Red Hots, I, Callie Anderson, was ready to attend my first dance!

"What should I say to him in drama? Should I ask him then? Maybe I could tell him how much I liked the poems he wrote in English last year. Here"—I shoved my lunch tray across the table to Ana, who had forgotten to bring her lunch—"take this. I'm so nervous I can't even eat."

Ana picked up the cold slice of pizza and began eating it hungrily.

"Do you think you'll go to the dance?" From all the admiring glances she received, Ana could probably ask a handful of different boys and they'd all say yes.

Ana swallowed a mouthful of pizza and said, "I don't really like dances." She paused and then added quickly, "And I don't know if you should ask Scott to the dance. What did Ellen say when you showed her the note?"

"I . . . I'll talk to her in drama class," I said, realizing I *hadn't* shown the note to Ellen earlier. It wasn't deliberate.

By the time I finished putting everything back in my locker, math class had already started. And then after Mrs. Faber dismissed us, Ellen and I had just gone our separate ways.

He still hadn't looked at me.

Scott spent the first half of drama class talking to Charlie while they sorted through a few trunks of props—without even one glance my way. Mr. Angelo had decreed today a work day and asked us to divide up into our backstage crews. But I had ditched Ana and the rest of the paint crew, who were working onstage, so I could hang out with Ellen and Stacy while they stitched sequins onto the Cinderella costume. Stacy had been chattering all period about her date for Sadie Hawkins, so I hadn't had a chance to talk to Ellen about Scott.

I'd opened the hallowed box of Red Hots and made a show of eating them. But Scott never noticed. The only person who *had* noticed was Ellen, who snapped that I'd better not get red stains all over "her" dress.

I kept eating them anyway. They soothed my stomach, which felt queasy with a mixture of anticipation and dread. I really wanted to ask Scott to the dance, but what if he said no? Then again, why would he say no? He'd sent me the Red Hots in the first place, right?

"He said he'd just been waiting for*ever* for me to ask him," Stacy was going on.

"Ouch!" I'd been so busy looking at Scott, but trying not to *look* like I was looking at Scott, that I stuck myself with the needle. I shook my finger, and then stuck it in my mouth, swallowing the metallic taste of blood.

"I told you not to get candy stains on my dress," Ellen snapped, pointing to a red splotch on the white fabric.

"That's not candy, that's blood," I snapped back, showing her my finger. "And unless you take that needle and stitch me up yourself, there's nothing I can do about it."

"Sorry," Ellen said, softening her tone. Then she glanced again at my finger and smiled. "Hey—remember the time we both nicked ourselves with my mother's sewing needles?" Ellen turned to an unsmiling Stacy. "We wanted to be blood sisters. But Callie tripped and practically took off a finger. We ran to my mom and told her—before she would even look at Callie's finger she asked if we got blood on her carpet."

"Yeah," I said, remembering. "Pinkies are a lot easier, don't you think?" I held mine out. "Best friends forever."

Ellen started to raise her pinkie, and then hesitated, making me wish I'd put on my glasses. Before I could reach for them, Stacy butted in.

"So, Ellen, did you tell Callie yet?" Stacy set down her needle and sequins.

Ellen lowered her arm, and her eyes, and a flush spread across her cheeks. While Ellen remained silent, I slipped my glasses from my backpack and put them on. I figured this would be a spy-worthy conversation.

"What's up?"

The air shimmered and the screen launched up next to Stacy: *Ellen never called her! I guess I'm Ellen's best friend now. Forget that stupid little pinkie squeeze.*

"Ellen likes someone," Stacy said smugly.

"Okay," I said. "Who is it?" I felt hurt that Ellen had talked to Stacy first, but I also felt excited. Maybe we could both ask someone to the dance and all go together. Take *that*, Stacy, you prissy little best-friend stealer!

Ellen looked up and said, "Scott Fowler. He's totally cute."

"Scott Fowler?" I repeated. A numbing sensation began spreading through my chest. Had I heard wrong? Ellen thought Scott—and his ponytail—were scruffy. When did Scott stop being scruffy, and become cute? "Since when have you ever cared about Scott Fowler?" My voice sounded like Ellen had done something wrong, but I couldn't help it. Scott Fowler had been my crush since forever. What right did Ellen have to him?

It wasn't fair. If Ellen really were Cinderella she wouldn't even need a fairy godmother to help her snag the Prince. She was already pretty, *and* smart, *and* she made friends easily. Why should she get Scott, too?

Ellen giggled, and a screen appeared next to her. I stared at the image inside: Ellen riding the Ferris wheel with Scott and laughing while he talked. It occurred to me that when Scott and I rode the Swisher together at the carnival, we'd both been pretty quiet. It's hard to talk when you're on a roller coaster.

I'd been so sure that Scott liked me. He'd sent me those Red Hots. That meant something, right?

But the note on the Red Hots was anonymous, I reminded myself. It could've been from anyone. Maybe there had been a mistake somewhere. Maybe I didn't have a secret admirer, after all.

"Ellen wants to ask Scott to the Sadie Hawkins dance." Stacy said it triumphantly, like she was so proud Ellen told her first.

"Oh. That's a good idea." I hung my head and sewed on another sequin. I wanted to believe that if Ellen and I both asked Scott to the dance, he'd pick me. But that was the thing about having a best friend who was pretty *and* smart *and* outgoing: They never did pick you. In image-conscious middle school Ellen was pure gold, and I felt like less than a dirty penny. In my head I could imagine Scott dancing with Ellen onstage in her sparkling Cinderella dress, and then whisking her off to the Sadie Hawkins dance like she was a real princess.

"I want to ask him," Ellen said. "But not if he's just going to say no."

I kept my head down, and kept sewing. After years of being Ellen's best friend, I knew where this conversation was going.

"So, I was wondering, could you find out for me?" Ellen asked. "You seem to just know things. I don't know how, but I swear, sometimes I think you can read minds. You could find out if he'd say yes. Scott likes you, you know. He told me he thinks you're funny."

Funny. Not beautiful, or smart, or even cute. Just funny. I looked over to the corner. Scott laughed as Charlie pulled a red wig from the trunk and stuck it on his head.

"Please, Callie. Do this for me, please? Best friends forever, right?" Now Ellen held her pinkie out. Instead of holding mine out, I looked at the screen hovering next to her and read her thoughts: *What's her problem? I'm just asking her to do one tiny little thing.*

Tiny little thing? *Whatever.* She could've just asked me to stuff my heart in her Cinderella costume so she could assault it with her sewing needles.

"I don't know. What would I say to him?"

"Ask him if he's going to the dance. Act casual, like you're just making conversation."

"What if he thinks I'm trying to ask him out myself?"

"He won't," Ellen said. *Callie, ask a guy out? Yeah, right.*

Two minutes ago I'd been preparing to do exactly that. Before Her Royal Highness Ellen chose the worst time ever to start talking to me about boys. What happened to her secretly thinking that "Callie wouldn't understand"?

"And then if he says he's not going to the dance," Ellen was saying, "you could say I wanted to go, but I wasn't sure who to ask."

I wished with all my heart I'd stayed with the paint crew today. Why did I think I needed Ellen's advice to ask Scott out, anyway? Miss *Über*confident herself wasn't going to personally risk rejection—she was like a general sending in the infantry to get shot down before swooping in to claim victory.

"Please, Callie?" Ellen asked, pinkie still raised.

I looked over at Stacy, and read her thoughts: *If Callie won't do it, then I will. That'll show Ellen who her best friend really is.*

"All right, I'll do it," I said, crossing my pinkie with Ellen's just as Stacy opened her mouth.

"Great," Ellen said. Something in her expression changed then, and she said, "Didn't you used to have a little crush on Scott last year?"

Little crush? Did she listen to me at all? I considered saying yes and that I still liked him, and if she didn't mind, *I'd* like to ask Scott to the dance.

But I knew I couldn't do that. Being a best friend meant that, sometimes, you were the infantry. And maybe, if I found out Scott didn't like Ellen back, I'd have a chance. Maybe he'd say he liked me and wanted to go to the dance with me.

And maybe, Ellen actually wouldn't be mad about that.

"You don't still like him, do you?" Ellen asked when I hesitated. But the screen bobbing next to her, showing me her thoughts, told me Ellen wasn't interested in hearing the truth: *Say no, Callie. Geez, just say no. What's taking her so long?*

"Ellen," Mr. Angelo called from the stage, "could you come up here for a minute?"

Ellen and I both stood up. "I don't like him," I said, taking my glasses off and tucking them into my back pocket. "I'll find out and let you know."

★ ★ ★

From the stage, Ana gave me a knowing smile as I walked toward Scott and Charlie. I smiled back thinly. She probably thought I was approaching Scott to ask him out myself.

Charlie pulled an oversize pair of plastic black glasses from the trunk, stuck them on his face, and fluffed his red wig. "Hey, Polka Dot, check it out. We're twins!"

"Funny." I looked away, glad he couldn't read my mind—because it was full of nasty thoughts. I didn't need to be reminded about my glasses and frizzy hair. Not right now.

"What's up?" Scott asked, picking through a trunk.

"Not much. I need a prop for Stacy. Something Wicked Stepmother worthy," I said, crouching down next to him and opening another trunk.

"I'll help. What does she want?" Charlie asked, taking off the glasses and wig.

"Oh, just whatever," I said, turning away from him and looking at Scott. "By the way, someone stuck a box of Red Hots in my locker this morning."

"Oh yeah? How'd they do that?" Scott looked interested. I couldn't tell if he really wanted to know, or if he was being flirty.

"Did you enjoy them?" Charlie asked softly.

"Sure," I said distractedly, focusing on Scott. "I loved them."

"Charlie," Mr. Angelo called from the stage, "could you come up here, please?"

Behind me I heard Charlie take off his wig and glasses and slam them back into the trunk. "I'll just leave you two alone," he said, and stalked away.

"He's been acting weird all day," Scott said.

I nodded and looked out at the multipurpose room as I reached back in my pocket for my glasses, and slipped them on.

The air shimmered and blue screens launched up around everyone. Mr. Angelo coached Ellen and Charlie onstage.

"Brilliant, Charlie. You're a natural. But Ellen, you need to put some emotion in it," Mr. Angelo said. "This isn't a book report, you know. *Feel* Cinderella. Feel her character. Feel the emotion. You need to remember your objective."

"All right, Mr. Angelo. I get it," Ellen said. From her thoughts though, it was clear she didn't get it. *Right now, my objective is to get off this stupid stage and away from my annoying teacher.*

Next to Ellen, Charlie grimaced, and I read his thoughts: *Forget it. She's too wrapped up in Scott to listen to anyone. Why did you even try?*

I suppressed a smile. I felt bad for thinking it, but a

part of me felt happy that Mr. Angelo—and Charlie—thought Ellen wasn't doing well in drama. Then I turned back to Scott. Time for the moment of truth.

"So, Ellen and I were talking about the Sadie Hawkins dance."

"Oh yeah? Have you guys asked anyone yet?" Words scrolled across the screen that launched up next to him: *She's so pretty. I wish she'd ask me.*

I blinked and wrapped my fingers around the trunk handle for support. Did Scott mean Ellen, or me? A part of me wanted to raise my hand, jump up and down, and shout, "Pick me, pick me, pick me!"

"No, I—we—haven't," I said, gripping the trunk handle tighter. "Any suggestions?"

Scott shrugged, but the screen hovering next to him showed me what I needed to know: Scott and Ellen dancing close together. Scott leaning toward Ellen, and Ellen leaning toward Scott . . .

I squeezed the trunk handle tighter and tighter. If I squeezed that handle hard enough, I could keep my voice from wavering and my eyes from watering.

What had I been thinking? Why would someone like Scott like someone like me? Especially when he could have someone like Ellen?

Scott's thoughts changed then: *Dude, she's got that death-stare thing going on again. Totally creepy.*

I squeezed the handle so hard my hand hurt.

"Okay, nice talking to you," I said. I stood up and slunk back to Stacy and Ellen, who had just been released from the stage.

"What did he say?" Ellen asked eagerly.

I smiled so widely I probably sprained a mouth muscle. "Go for it. He'll say yes."

With an excited giggle, Ellen headed over to Scott.

When I turned back to Stacy, she had a strange look on her face. And her thoughts were even stranger: *Oh, I get it. Callie liked him. I remember that. I remember when they never liked me back.*

What did Stacy remember? Who never liked her back? I ripped off my glasses and tossed them onto my backpack. I was so sick of reading people's thoughts. Most of the time, their thoughts were just as confusing as their words. And I was tired of it. I stomped over to the paint crew; they were busy with a scene from the ball.

"Hi, Callie," Gretchen said. "Can you help me? I'm having trouble mixing the colors again."

"Later, okay?" I said as I plopped down next to Ana. "He never liked me," I whispered to her. "He liked Ellen all along."

Ana was silent. Then she handed me a brush and said, "*Pintura conmigo*. Paint with me."

I grabbed the brush. After I'd made a few strokes I heard her say softly, "*Él es muy estúpido*. Scott is very stupid."

"You're right," I said. "He *is* very stupid."

And then I began to cry.

Chapter 14

✦ ✦ ✦

Super Freaky Glasses Rule #13
Some gifts you just can't get rid of.
No matter how hard you try.

"Dr. Ingram will see you now."

I nodded at Mrs. Dillard and heaved myself off the plushy red velvet sofa. Mom had needed to pick something up at the teacher supply store. Instead of hanging out in the doughnut shop, I told her I wanted to stop by Dr. Ingram's and see if my glasses had arrived.

When I entered the examination room, Dr. Ingram was polishing his glasses.

"Callie, what a nice surprise. Unfortunately, your glasses are still on back order. Normally, it wouldn't take this long, but this seems to be a special case. If you would kindly sit down." Dr. Ingram gestured to the exam chair, like he was inviting me in for tea or something.

"No. I don't want to sit." I pointed behind him, where framed diplomas hung on the wall. "Just what kind of a doctor are you, anyway?"

Dr. Ingram looked surprised as he put his glasses back on. "I'm a doctor who helps people see. I would have thought that was quite obvious."

"Oh yeah?" I held up my glasses. "Do you have any idea what *I've* seen the past two months? These glasses are making my life miserable."

"Really, how so?" Dr. Ingram squinted at me through his glasses, and I wondered, *Did his glasses have magic powers like mine?*

"Are you reading my thoughts right now?" I asked.

Dr. Ingram hesitated. "You're angry and quite upset with me."

"Ha, I knew it! You *can* read my thoughts."

"Not at all. It doesn't take a mind reader, or even a particularly observant person, to see that you're angry. What I'm wondering is why?"

"Why? Are you kidding? Ever since you gave me these stupid glasses my life has just gotten worse." I held the glasses out to Dr. Ingram. "Take them back."

"I'm sorry. I'm afraid I cannot."

"Why not?"

"Because the glasses you hold are truly special. Everyone I've ever loaned them to has developed a strange connection to them. Though I must confess, I'm not sure why. I've found that the recipients of those glasses need them in more ways than they originally imagined."

I didn't believe him. I think he knew exactly what my glasses could do. "You knew something was up with my glasses. You even told me to use them wisely."

"I see. And did you?"

"Did I what?"

"Use them wisely?"

"Does it matter?"

"Of course it matters," Dr. Ingram said. "Some gifts are given to us that we may learn, not so we won't suffer. And some of the best gifts in the world are those that first cause us pain."

I walked farther into the office and sank into the examination chair. Somehow, I didn't think "using the glasses wisely" meant using them to keep your best friend, or trying to find out who your crush liked. Although they definitely qualified in the painful department.

"What is it you want me to learn?" I asked, leaning my

head back against the cool leather. "You tell me to use the glasses wisely, but I don't even know what that means. How can I understand anything you say when you always speak in puzzles?

"If you've got some grand plan for these glasses," I continued, "then you should've given them to someone else. Someone smarter. Someone braver. Someone who could make a difference."

"Who's to say *you* aren't that someone?" Dr. Ingram said softly. "Sometimes vision correction takes time. Fear not, Calliope Meadow Anderson. I am sure the glasses will reveal their purpose in due course. For it's not that I have 'some grand plan,' as you say, for these glasses. But perhaps these glasses have some grand plan for you."

"Whatever," I said. "You're talking in puzzles again."

The bell jingled, and I stood up at the sound of Mom's voice.

"Promise me you'll think about what I said," Dr. Ingram said as I turned to leave.

"I promise." I hesitated, and then asked, "Ellen tried on my glasses. How come she couldn't see what I see?"

Dr. Ingram thought for a second. "I suppose there are those who see, and those who do not want to see."

My optometrist, the philosopher.

As I walked out the door, I heard Dr. Ingram grumbling to himself. "One thing I always liked about that Cinderella. She was always so thankful to *her* fairy godmother."

I said good-bye to Mrs. Dillard then, and made a decision: Next time I needed to get my eyes checked, I was heading to the mall.

Chapter 15

✢ ✢ ✢

Super Freaky Glasses Rule #14
One very unwise use of the glasses: spying on people when they're lost in Coupleland. Can you say ewww?

WHEN YOUR BEST FRIEND GETS HER FIRST BOYFRIEND, IT'S a total bummer. Especially when you have a crush on said boyfriend. Ellen had always been time conscious, but now she took it to a whole new level. Our conversations were all about minutes now. How many minutes Ellen spent on the phone with Scott. How many minutes until Ellen got to see Scott. How many minutes since Ellen had last seen Scott.

Oh, and get *this*: Scott wrote Ellen poetry. That's right. Last year, I dreamed about receiving a romantic haiku from Scott. This year, Ellen actually did.

We had conversations about Scott. We had conversations about Scott's feelings. We had conversations about Ellen's feelings about Scott's feelings.

Scott and Ellen had been dating for a few weeks, and they were practically one person now. In my head (and in the stories I wrote), I secretly called them Scotlen.

Scott and Ellen walked each other to class, ate lunch together, and hung all over each other in drama class. I started sitting with Ana in drama, safely away from Scotlen's lovesick aura.

"Don't look at them," Ana advised me one day after we'd taken seats on the floor of the multipurpose room to practice our lines.

"I'm not looking at them."

"I'm just saying. They're being all—what are the words you said?—flirty faced. They're being flirty faced, yes?"

"How would I know if they're being flirty faced? I'm not looking at them, remember?" I glanced across the room. Stacy and Charlie—both of them looking uncomfortable and slightly embarrassed—sat on either side of Scott and Ellen, who giggled at a private joke. "Yep. They're being flirty faced. It's totally disgusting."

Ana grinned. "Like, totally, for sure."

We cracked up, and I felt a little better. Ana and I ate

lunch together more often, on account of me feeling the urge to barf whenever I ate with Scotlen. On the days Ana wasn't tutoring me in Spanish, I'd started tutoring her in the all-important tongue of California Valley Girl.

I peeked over at Ellen and Scott again and pulled my glasses out of my backpack. *Use your glasses wisely.* I'd been thinking about what that meant, but after a few weeks, I still had no clue.

I slipped the glasses on. The air shimmered and the screens appeared, showing me Scotlen's dopey love thoughts. Yuck. Definitely not a wise use of the glasses.

"I told you not to look at them," Ana said.

"I'm not looking at them." I turned my attention back to my script.

Ana nudged my shoulder and said, "Look."

I turned, and saw Stacy walking toward us with a tentative smile on her face.

"Can I sit with you guys?" she asked.

"Why?" I blurted out, and then heard Ana hiss, *"Callie!"* in a disapproving tone of voice.

Stacy didn't say anything, but the air shimmered, and a screen sprang up next to her and a couple of images flashed by: of Stacy in the cafeteria, quietly eating her lunch while Ellen and Scott giggled next to her. Then of Stacy looking bored in Ellen's room while Ellen talked on the phone (to Scott, I figured).

I moved my backpack. "I mean . . . sure, sit down."

"Thanks." Stacy sounded relieved.

"So how are things over in Coupleland?" I asked.

"Oh, you know, it's sort of like *The Scott and Ellen Show*."

We all turned to look at Scotlen—who continued to flirt and giggle. Charlie smiled at us, looked at Scott and Ellen, and rolled his eyes. Then he pretended to choke himself. Ana, Stacy, and I busted up laughing.

"Girls! Are you practicing your lines?" Mr. Angelo asked.

"Yes, Mr. Angelo," we answered, and went back to our scripts.

We studied our lines silently, and I looked up when I heard Ana sigh. I wasn't trying to spy on her thoughts. But I had the glasses on, and by now it was just habit.

The air shimmered, and the blue screen appeared. Inside was an image of Ana and me, and a few other girls from school—girls from Ana's ESL class, I thought. We were in a diner eating hamburgers and french fries and chocolate shakes. Ana and I had never gone out for hamburgers before—so this couldn't be one of her memories. Was it a daydream, I wondered, staring at the faraway look on Ana's face. Was Ana wishing she were somewhere else instead of drama class?

She wouldn't be the only one, I thought, glancing around the room and reading the screens hovering next to the other students. It was Friday afternoon, and with only ten minutes to go until the bell rang, mostly everyone had moved on from drama class. Mentally, anyway.

I peeked at Scotlen again and saw they were still lost in Dopesville. Ellen was daydreaming about Scott while *I* had a weekend of nothing to look forward to except my mom's Post-it notes of chores. But it didn't have to be that way, right? I didn't have to spend the weekend sitting around waiting for Ellen to call. I looked over at Stacy. Ellen had made new friends this year. I could too. And I wasn't going to feel guilty about it anymore.

"Hey," I whispered to Ana. "Do you want to hang out this weekend? Maybe my mom could drop us off at the movies, and we could get hamburgers or something afterward?"

In the screen hovering next to Ana the image of the diner vanished and was replaced by tons of Spanish words scrolling across. Ana looked surprised, and I thought she was about to smile. But then her expression changed, and she said, "I can't. I have a lot of homework this weekend."

"Come on, it could be a lot of fun. Like totally, *por favor*?"

I thought it was funny, combining Spanish and California Valley Girl, and I purposely said it to make her laugh.

But Ana stared at me like I'd just spoken Chinese. "No." Her voice reminded me of steel—hard and unbending.

"Oh, okay, no problem," I said, backing off quickly and looking down at my script. Sometimes I felt like Ana and I were friends, like when we ate lunch together or hung out in drama class. But sometimes—like right then—I wondered if she was just being nice to me because we were neighbors.

A few days later, I felt like a vandal, even though I stood in front of my own locker. Twenty minutes had passed since the final bell rang; twenty minutes I spent hiding in the bathroom, trying not to look like a weirdo, while girls breezed in and out to gossip or apply lip gloss. Finally, certain Raven had left for the day, I'd escaped the bathroom and headed for our locker.

Use your glasses wisely, Dr. Ingram's voice rang in my mind. Finally, I thought I'd found one way to use them wisely.

Furtively looking down the hall, I slipped on my glasses, took a blue flyer from my backpack, and opened my locker. Then I did the unthinkable.

I touched Raven's stuff.

Her English textbook rested at the bottom of the locker, along with a broken pencil, some dusty Red Hots, and a couple of homework assignments I thought I'd lost. I grabbed the textbook and scanned the flyer one last time:

RESOURCE TESTING AND TUTORING.

I'd found it in the library a few days before. Ellen had a club meeting during lunch, and Ana had been absent that day, so I'd avoided the cafeteria completely and spent the hour hanging out in the library. The flyer advertised a program designed for students diagnosed with dyslexia.

The librarian had come up and asked me if I needed any help.

"What's dyslexia?" I'd asked. "I've heard of it, but I'm not sure what it means."

"It's a learning disability," she'd said. "It makes it difficult for someone to read—they have trouble interpreting letters and words."

I wished Raven had seen the flyer. I didn't know if she had dyslexia. But from spying on her thoughts I did know she got herself kicked out of English class earlier that day because she felt too terrified to read out loud.

The librarian asked me if I would like to take one, and I had said no, I was only looking at it because of a friend.

"Oh, a friend. I see." She had given me a knowing smile, like she was keeping a secret, then handed me a flyer. "Well, maybe your friend would like one."

Now I folded up the flyer and glanced once more down the hall. Then with trembling hands I opened the textbook. If Raven caught me—

"Callie, hello!"

I jumped and spun around, smacking into Mrs. Faber and the ginormous shoulder bag she carried. Raven's textbook tumbled to the floor with a loud *thunk*.

"Sorry, Mrs. Faber," I said, reaching down and retrieving the textbook.

"No problem. I meant to tell you earlier, you did a great job in class today."

"Thanks," I said, hoping she'd leave. Earlier in the morning it seemed like Mrs. Faber had gone out of her way to ask me a gazillion questions—even though I never once raised my hand. All of which I answered correctly, thanks to my super freaky magic glasses.

Mrs. Faber began rummaging through her shoulder bag. "I was going to give this back to you tomorrow morning, but . . ." She pulled out a paper and handed it to me.

It was my latest homework assignment, inked in red with a huge C.

"Callie, are you feeling under challenged in my class?"

I looked at the paper, and then back at Mrs. Faber. "Huh?"

"What I mean is, does the homework bore you? Or is this class too easy? Perhaps we should discuss moving you to advanced algebra? Because no matter when I call on you, you always know the right answer. And yet your homework—when you bother to turn it in—shows a definite lack of attention."

Okay, I didn't know what to say to that. I was almost hoping Raven would appear and catch me touching her stuff. "I'm sorry, Mrs. Faber," I said. "I guess sometimes I just forget."

The air shimmered and a screen sprang up next to Mrs. Faber: *Something's not right. Half the time she isn't even paying attention in class—so how does she know the answer when I make her participate? And those glasses. She's always taking them off and putting them back on and staring at her classmates. That kind of behavior just doesn't seem normal.*

"Um, Mrs. Faber, I really have to get home soon," I said. "But I'll try harder, I promise."

"You do that, Calliope."

I caught the last of Mrs. Faber's thoughts as she left: *I wonder if maybe she's really gifted, and doesn't want anyone to know? Oh well, I'll continue asking her questions, and if this keeps up, I can ask to have her tested next semester.*

Right then I made a mental note to myself. Effective immediately: answer all questions in math class incorrectly.

Before anyone else could interrupt, I quickly tucked the flyer into Raven's textbook, wedged it back into our locker, and shut the door.

Another glance up and down the hallway, and I sighed with relief. I hadn't been caught. Maybe when Raven opened her book in English class tomorrow she'd see the flyer and think it was a sign or something. Maybe someone would help her, and she could stop feeling so scared all the time.

Chapter 16

✫　✫　✫

Super Freaky Glasses Rule #15
Not everyone has a pair of magic glasses. If you're sorry for something, they won't know unless you say so.

"Want some chocolate?" Ellen said a couple weeks later in drama class. "They're from Scott."

I looked at the gooey sweets she offered my way and tried not to gag. I was so *not* going to eat Scott's latest love declaration. I didn't care how good those truffles smelled.

"No thanks," I said, staring at the truffle and the dreamy expression on Ellen's face. "Too much sweetness makes me barf."

Stacy stifled a giggle, but Ellen seemed unfazed.

"Your loss." Ellen popped the truffle into her mouth.

"Anyway, then he said I was pretty, and then he said he had a crush on me in sixth grade, and then he said—"

"That he would've asked you out last year, but you never noticed him. Yes, Ellen, I *know*."

I wasn't wearing my glasses. That's not how I knew what Ellen was going to say. I knew because Ellen told me this story twice already. Once before first period started. Then again after first period ended. And now in drama, when we were supposed to be running our lines.

"Come on," I said, cutting off Ellen, who was still slobbering on and on about Scott. "The play is this weekend. We need to practice."

"What's to practice?" Ellen said. "It's just memorizing a bunch of words—it's like taking a test."

"It's not at all like taking a test," I said. "You have to learn your character."

"Sheesh, Callie, you sound just as bad as Mr. Angelo." Scott came up behind Ellen, followed by a glum-looking Charlie. Scott struck a pose and said in his best Mr. Angelo impersonation, "You have to *learn* your character. You have to *feel* your character. You have to *respect* your character."

Ellen giggled and Scott continued. "I think you've practiced with your understudy enough for one day, don't you? Want to hang out with your Prince?"

"Sure."

"Wait, Ellen, don't you think . . ." I trailed off as Ellen and Scott floated away to the corner, where they sat down and started whispering.

"It's no use," Charlie said behind me. "They don't take it seriously. And they're both horrible actors."

I laughed and turned around. "Don't hold back, tell me how you really feel."

Charlie grinned and shrugged. "It's true. Every time I've practiced with her she hasn't done much more than just recite her lines. To tell you the truth"—he lowered his voice—"I was surprised Ellen got the lead. I mean, I know she's your best friend and all, but I really thought you'd be Cinderella."

"You did?"

"Yeah, I thought your audition was hilarious."

"I'm sure Mr. Angelo had a good reason for giving the part to Ellen," I said, choosing my words carefully. "Besides, why do you care? You said you were just taking drama to get an easy A."

I thought about the few times I'd spied on Charlie's thoughts—he was usually reciting his lines in his head. "You were lying, weren't you? You actually like drama."

Charlie grinned. "Don't tell Scott."

I nodded and turned away and realized that I just had a whole conversation with a boy without getting nervous or using my glasses to talk to him.

Weird.

I sat down next to Stacy, who flipped a page in her script so hard it tore, making a loud ripping sound. She stared at Ellen and Scott with a strange expression on her face, so I slipped my glasses out of my backpack and waited until the screen appeared next to her: *What good is having a best friend if she's never around? Ellen hasn't called me all week.*

I knew how Stacy felt—it had been weeks since Ellen called me regularly. And now that I thought about it, I never saw Stacy hang out with anyone else other than Ellen.

Kind of like me.

"Callie. Stacy." Mr. Angelo stalked over to us, looking irritated. "What are you two doing?"

"Nothing," we both answered.

"Precisely. If you can't be bothered to practice your lines, then perhaps I could trouble you to run an errand instead."

"Okay," Stacy said. "We'll do it." *I have to get out of here,* her thoughts scrolled across the screen hovering next to her.

I know exactly how you feel, I wanted to tell her.

"Here's a hall pass. Take these receipts to Principal

Reynolds's office." Mr. Angelo handed Stacy a stack of slips.

We left, and I read the thoughts scrolling across the screen bobbing along next to Stacy: *I sooooo cannot stand another minute of Scott and Ellen. They make me sick. She missed the Key Club meeting because she couldn't bear to be away from him. I only joined that lame club because she did.*

We continued to walk, and the silence became uncomfortable until Stacy said, "What are you doing tomorrow after school?"

"My dad is taking my sister and me out to dinner." Finally Dad said he could come down early for the weekend. Mom had gone out of her way to be nice to him all week whenever they talked on the phone.

"Oh." Stacy looked away, and the words scrolling across the screen changed: *Great. So I have to go out for pizza with* The Scott and Ellen Show *by myself tomorrow. Fun.*

I looked away, grateful Stacy hadn't said anything out loud. I didn't want to tell her Ellen hadn't mentioned anything to me about going out for pizza.

After we dropped the receipts off at Principal Reynolds's office and headed back to drama, we heard a stern voice echoing down the hall.

"Hey, you!" A boy as skinny as a lima bean, and clad in

the blue and gold vest all hall monitors were required to wear, flagged us down.

"What are you doing out of class?" The air shimmered, and the blue screen appeared next to him. *They are so busted*, his thoughts said.

"We're running errands for our teacher." Stacy fished the hall pass out of her pocket and showed it to him.

He glanced at it suspiciously. "This doesn't look like a teacher's handwriting."

"Would you like to walk us back to class and talk to Mr. Angelo?" Stacy asked in her sweetest voice.

He thrust the pass back at Stacy. "Just don't dawdle."

Stacy and I waited until he'd turned the corner to burst into giggles. "What a creep," she said.

"I know," I said. "Hey—did you know at the beginning of the year Ellen wanted to be a hall monitor?"

"No. Did you, too?"

"No. I told her people would run away from us."

"And what did Ellen say to that?"

"That only the slackers would run away."

Stacy laughed. "That sounds like Ellen."

We continued down the hall, and Stacy's thoughts changed: An image formed, of me and Ellen and Stacy eating lunch one day in the cafeteria. Ellen and Stacy were giggling over a joke or something. And when I looked at myself, I realized I was glaring. Right at Stacy. Then another image—of me and Stacy and Ana sitting together in drama class, the day I asked Ana to go to the movies. While I whispered to Ana, Stacy looked at us hopefully. But when I went back to my script, her smile vanished.

Had Stacy been hoping I would invite her, too?

The screen changed again, and Stacy's thoughts scrolled across: *I wish Callie didn't hate me so much.*

I almost smacked into a row of lockers. I didn't hate Stacy. I just didn't like her a whole lot. Weren't you supposed to dislike the girl who stole your best friend? Then again, how did I know I didn't like Stacy? I barely knew her. And that was my fault, I realized. Stacy had tried to be friends with me at the beginning of the year—she even offered to help me paint my room. I'd always found a way to ignore her. But I could change that, I decided. Starting now.

"So, what was it like in Oregon?" I asked.

Stacy shrugged and said nothing. But in the screen hovering next to her I saw something unexpected. A picture of Green Braces Girl. But this time, I really, *really* looked at her.

And I realized that girl was Stacy.

She was about twenty pounds heavier, wore no makeup, and had dull hair instead of her current golden locks. But it was Stacy, no doubt about it. The picture kept changing: first Green Braces Girl, Stacy, sat alone in a school cafeteria. Then alone in a classroom while groups of students around her talked and laughed. The images continued, showing Stacy exercising, dying her hair, and finally getting her braces removed, all while she counted the weeks off on a calendar to a day with the note "Moving" written in thick red marker. The last image showed Stacy—the way she looked now—smiling widely as Ellen sat down next to her in science class and started chatting.

"It was okay," Stacy said finally. "But I like it better here."

I nodded. I wasn't mad at Stacy for stealing Ellen away anymore, I realized. After seeing her thoughts, I could understand why she'd want a best friend.

I wanted to tell Stacy I was sorry for ever being a jerk to her—but the words just wouldn't come. Maybe though, I could do something else. "Did I hear Ellen say something about going out for pizza after school tomorrow?"

Stacy nodded, and I continued, "I'm not seeing my dad until later—so maybe I could meet you there. We could watch an episode of *The Scott and Ellen Show* together."

Stacy smiled. "That would be great, Callie. Really, really great."

We walked the rest of the way back to class, and I read more of Stacy's thoughts: *Maybe Callie and I can become friends after all.*

Maybe, I thought back at her. *Stranger things have happened.*

Chapter 17

☆ ☆ ☆

Super Freaky Glasses Rule #16

Don't expect your magic glasses to figure out your own thoughts. That's your job.

THE SCOTT AND ELLEN SHOW GOT REALLY OLD, REALLY fast the next afternoon at the pizza place. So Stacy, Ana, and I finally moved to another booth. When I invited Ana the night before, I figured she would just say no, so I was surprised when she agreed to come.

"No," Ana said to Stacy. "No, it's '*Es major que no llores.*' Try it again." While we waited for our pizza, Ana was trying to teach Stacy to sing "Santa Claus is Coming to Town" in Spanish. Stacy kept getting the words wrong, and would laugh so hard soda snorted from her nose, which would cause Ana to laugh so hard soda snorted from *her* nose.

I didn't feel like singing so I just watched them quietly, and wound a paper napkin around my thumb until my skin turned white.

"Are you okay?" Stacy asked.

"Yeah, my stomach just hurts," I said, loosening the napkin. "I'm hungry." That was partly a lie, though. My stomach *did* hurt—but not because I was hungry.

"I'll find out what's taking the pizza so long," Stacy said. "Want to come?" she asked Ana, who nodded.

After they left I glanced over at Scott and Ellen, who were sitting next to each other and playing a game on Scott's cell phone. Then I leaned my head against the glass window. Outside, cars splashed through puddles of rain and the streetlights looked fuzzy, like angels with colorful halos. It was warm and steamy inside the pizza place, but I felt something icy gripping my stomach.

I always figured if I never told Ellen—or anyone else—about Mom and Dad's problems, then in a way, they didn't exist. I could pretend that Dad really *was* away working somewhere, and there was no one to tell me any different. Tonight though I would see him for the first time in months, and I wasn't so sure I could pretend anymore.

Stacy slid into the booth and placed our pepperoni pizza on the table. Ana slid in next to me.

"Are you sure you're okay?" Stacy asked, handing me a slice of pizza.

"You look upset," Ana added.

I thought about giving them my usual answer, and telling them I was fine. But I felt words bubbling up inside me. Words I wanted to say out loud.

"My parents don't always get along," I said hesitantly. Stacy and Ana waited while I took a bite of pizza. I swallowed. "So my mom kicked my dad out of the house. He's been living in northern California. I'm actually seeing him tonight."

"Hey, are you guys all right over there?" came Ellen's voice. She had detached herself from Scott, and was looking over at our table with a frown.

Stacy glanced at me, and I shook my head. "Yeah, we're fine," she called back.

Ana squeezed my shoulder and asked, "How long has he been gone?"

"Since August."

"Since August?" Stacy repeated. "That's a long time."

"Yeah," I said, leaning my head back against the window. "It *is* a long time."

When I got home from the pizza place, I decided to write a story about my dad. It would be the best one I'd ever written. A story so great it would show him how much I missed him these last several months. He would be the star of my story, in one of the roles I usually gave him: a prince, a noble knight sworn to protect an ancient treasure, or a martial arts master fighting off a sea of enemies with his bare hands.

But as I sat in my window seat wearing my glasses and tapping my pencil against my journal, the words wouldn't come.

Behind me, I heard my door open and Mom say, "What are you doing? Your father will be here soon and the towels are still sitting on the couch. I told you to fold them before you leave."

"Are you physically incapable of knocking?" I snapped. Then I looked down at my journal and said, "I'm—writing an essay for English class."

Mom opened her mouth, and then closed it. But I knew what she almost said, because the screen appeared by her, and I saw her thoughts scrolling across: *She's not studying. She's got that same look on her face her father gets when he's lying to me. Maybe you should tell her—oh forget it—the last thing you need is a fight so she can tell Nathan how horrible you are.*

Sometimes I really hated wearing the glasses around Mom. A lot of days I felt like she didn't even see me. Even if she was looking right at me, she was too busy thinking about my dad to really see me. If Mom hated him so much (right now, anyway) and I reminded her of him, then how did she feel about me?

The words on the screen hovering next to Mom changed: *I need to clean the house before Nathan gets here. Remind him that Sarah is allergic to milk. Remind him about Callie's play. Should I change into something else?*

I watched Mom as her thoughts scrolled across the blue screen. She twisted a strand of hair around her finger, and had a faraway look in her eyes.

"Do you miss him?" I asked.

Mom lowered her arm. "Miss who?"

"Dad."

"He's your father, Calliope. Of course I miss him." But that's not what her thoughts said: *I miss the couple we used to be.*

I wondered what that meant. Were my parents different people now than when I was younger? Somehow I couldn't picture my mother, the person in front of me now, letting my dad name me Calliope Meadow. But she did, didn't she?

After Mom left, I took off my glasses and opened my closet. I wondered if I should change into something else too. What did you wear for a "Daddy Date" when you haven't seen your father in months? What was the right combination? What dress would say *please, come home*?

I used to be so excited for "Daddy Dates." An eager beaver, he called me. But now I felt all confused and twisty inside. A part of me couldn't wait for my dad to get here, but another part of me just wanted the night to be over.

I put my glasses back on. Then I looked in the mirror and waited. But no screen appeared beside my head. I sighed and took them off again.

What good was a pair of magic glasses if they couldn't even help you figure out your own thoughts?

The night didn't start well. First Sarah didn't want to go. She hugged Mom's legs, teary-eyed, until Dad said she could order a huge sundae for dessert.

"She most certainly can *not* have that for dessert," Mom said.

"Cheer up, Sleepy Jean. It's just one sundae. Let the kid live a little."

"She's allergic to dairy, Nathan. If you give her a sundae, her eyes will swell shut."

When we finally arrived at the restaurant, Dad got irritated over the long wait. His mood didn't improve when Sarah started whining that she would rather go to McDonald's.

Once we were finally seated and the waiter brought us ice water, Dad said, "So Callie Cat, have you written any stories about your poor old man?"

I started to tell Dad he wasn't old. But when I looked at him, he actually did seem older to me. His brown curls were streaked with gray, and there was a crease between his eyes I hadn't noticed last summer.

"I haven't written any lately," I answered instead.

"Oh, well, I guess you're too busy, what with the play tomorrow. Tell me again, what part are you playing?"

"I'm the understudy for Cinderella."

"Understudy? You mean you won't actually be onstage?" Dad frowned and the crease between his eyes grew deeper.

"Well, no. But I've helped Ellen—she's playing Cinderella—a lot. And I've painted a lot of the set pieces. I mix the colors just the way you taught me to."

"Speaking of paint, I've just finished some pieces I'm very proud of. Really, being in Napa has been wonderful for me."

"I paint too, Daddy," Sarah said. "Every day Miss Tammy lets me paint and she says—"

"Yes, I'm sure you're a great painter, Sarah Beara, just like your poor old dad. But the sights in Napa are inspiring. The hills are the greenest you've ever seen, and the trees look like big bushes of broccoli sprouting right out of the ground."

"Broccoli?" Sarah said, wrinkling her nose. "Ewwww."

"No, it's wonderful. And with Daddy's new job, it gives him tons of time to paint."

Dad flashed me his special smile, the one that usually lit me up inside. But this time it left me feeling cold. If he had a new job in Napa, did that mean he was planning to stay there for a while?

"What new job?" I asked in a small voice.

"I'm selling hotel furniture for a supplier up there."

The waiter came then to take our orders. Just as I opened my mouth to ask for spaghetti, Dad said, "I'll have the shrimp scampi, and the ladies will have the salmon." With a flourish, he handed the waiter our menus.

I'd forgotten how much Dad liked to order for us. I used to think it was so cool, how he'd go out of his way to order the most expensive item on the menu, and so what if I didn't like fish? I'd smoosh it around my plate so it looked like I'd eaten it. Dad never seemed to notice, and even if he did, he let me order chocolate cake for dessert anyway.

But this time, it didn't seem cool. It just seemed annoying. And maybe it showed on my face, because Dad said, "Really, Callie Cat, you're wearing your mother's scowl. It's quite unbecoming of you."

"Sorry." I fidgeted with my glasses, which I'd hidden on my lap under a napkin. There was one question I wanted to ask him—and I wanted the truth. With a deep breath, I pulled out the glasses and put them on.

The air waved and shimmered, the blue screen launched up by Dad, and his thoughts scrolled across: *What ghastly glasses. No wonder she hates them so much. I'll have to speak to Jean about that.*

I flinched, and tried not to get distracted. "So, Dad, when are you coming home? I mean, I'm sure if you asked, Mom would let you come back, just like last time."

"Um . . ." Dad paused. *What did Jean tell them?*

"Yeah, Daddy. When are you coming home?"

"Uh-oh." Dad looked away from me and smiled at Sarah. "Do I hear an echo bird in here, Sarah Beara?"

Sarah laughed. But I didn't. I stared at the screen hovering next to him, which held one sentence: *Did Jean tell them about Brenda?*

"Who's Brenda?" I asked.

Dad squirmed in his seat, and stared at the salt shaker

like it was the most fascinating thing in the world. *So she did tell her. Jean will do anything to make me look bad.*

"Yeah, Daddy. Who's Brenda?" Sarah asked. "See? I'm an echo bird."

Dad glanced at me, and then at Sarah. "Brenda is Daddy's special friend, Sarah Beara."

"I have a special friend too, Daddy. Her name is Milly Carson . . ."

I looked down at my hands as Sarah chattered away. Maybe I didn't know a lot about love and all that stuff. But I knew what it meant when your father told you he had a special friend named Brenda.

It meant, this time, he wasn't coming home.

"Is Brenda the reason why she kicked you out?" I asked, cutting Sarah off.

The words on the screen hovering near Dad changed: *Jean let them think she kicked me out? That was kind of her. Out of character, but kind.*

The screen changed and I saw an image of Dad packing a suitcase, while Mom stood by him, crying. She grabbed his arm, but he shook her off and kept packing.

"Yes, Callie Cat," Dad said, looking again at the salt shaker. "I suppose it was."

★　★　★

"How did it go?" Mom asked after she'd put Sarah to bed.

I shrugged and went back to the TV program I'd been watching. "Dad ordered for us."

"Oh. Fish, right?"

"Yeah."

Mom headed for the kitchen. "Then you must be hungry."

I slipped my glasses out from under the throw blanket I'd cuddled up under, put them on, and followed Mom into the kitchen.

"He's not coming back this time, is he?" I asked softly.

Mom silently layered deli meat on a piece of wheat bread. The screen appeared by her and I read her thoughts: *How do you tell your daughters their father just isn't the family type?*

"It's too early to tell," she said finally.

"Why did you let me think you kicked him out?"

Mom froze, a knife full of mustard raised in midair. She didn't even notice when a glob splatted onto the counter. "It was just easier that way," she said. But her thoughts said something else: *Because I know he's your favorite.*

"I'm not like him," I said. "I may like to write. And I like to paint like he does. But I'm not like him."

"I know that," Mom said in a husky voice. "I really do know that, Callie."

I watched Mom as she finished making the sandwich.

She was always here. She was the one who made dinner, and the one who took Sarah to the sitter's each morning before heading to work. The one who paid the Visa bill and wondered how she'd keep us all together. And I loved her for that. Maybe Mom hadn't seen me lately. But I hadn't seen her, either. Not really. Not for a long time.

Mom put the sandwich on a plate and passed it to me. "So what else did you and your father talk about?"

Why are you even asking her? The words scrolled across the screen. *She's not going to talk to you.*

I took the plate. And I decided I was going to try. "It went fine," I said, sitting down at the kitchen table. "Except at first, Sarah told Dad she wanted a Happy Meal."

Mom laughed. "I bet that went over real well."

I laughed too. "Yeah, she also told him her fish was stinky."

We talked for a while. When I went upstairs later, somehow I knew that although Mom and I would probably be fighting again tomorrow, we'd be okay.

Chapter 18

�֯ ✯ ✯

Super Freaky Glasses Rule #17
Know when it's time to take the glasses off.

TWO HOURS BEFORE THE PLAY STARTED I WAS TEARING MY room apart—trying to find my Cinderella script—when the phone rang.

"Callie!" came Mom's voice from downstairs. "Ana's on the phone for you."

I picked up my phone. "Hey—sorry I'm running late," I said, rummaging around my desk. "I just have to find my script and then I'll come over and we can walk to school."

"That is why I called," Ana said. "I woke up this morning with that flu that is going around. I cannot be in the play." Ana blew her nose loudly. "Sorry."

"You can't be in the play?" I asked. "But—"

"I already called Mr. Angelo and he said not to worry about it."

I sat down on my window seat and looked over at the Garcias' house. I wished I could see Ana inside. Her voice sounded strange. Not like she was sick. More like she was trying not to cry.

"Okay. But is everything all right? Because you sound—"

"I have to go, Callie. Tío needs to use the phone."

Ana hung up, and I decided to call her back after the play. Then I spent a few more minutes hunting for my script. Finally, I gave up. I was just Ellen's understudy. It wasn't like I'd actually need it.

Inside the multipurpose room, chaos reigned. Students scurried around, making last minute adjustments to costumes and set decorations. Scott set up rows of folding chairs. Mr. Angelo barked orders to a group of students while he checked the sound system. Raven yelled at a student who spilled water on her costume. Charlie paced back and forth in a corner, muttering his lines to himself.

Gretchen Baxter hurried over. "I'm so glad you're here. We need your help." Onstage, she showed me the pumpkin patch set piece—with a huge black splotch in the middle. "Scott accidentally kicked over the black paint. Mr. Angelo said we would just have to fix it and not worry if it didn't dry—but no one can mix the colors like you do."

"All right," I said, taking off my jacket and kneeling. "Get me a few rags and the yellow, orange, white, and brown paints." Gretchen and I, along with a few other students, set about fixing the scene.

"Callie!" Stacy said, hurrying up the stairs to the stage "I've been looking for you everywhere! You need to come backstage." She sounded annoyed and excited and panicked all at the same time.

"But we're not done yet," Gretchen protested, "and we still need Callie to—"

"Doesn't matter," Stacy said, cutting her off. "Mr. Angelo said Callie needs to go backstage. Right now."

"Ellen is sick, I don't think she'll be able to go on tonight," Stacy said after I handed Gretchen my paintbrush. "And Mr. Angelo said Ana can't make it, either. He asked me to take over her part. It's not a lot of lines, and the Fairy Godmother is never onstage with the Wicked Stepmother. Mr. Angelo asked me to try on Ana's costume, but I can't find the wand that goes with it."

Stacy led me backstage as she talked, past a group of students dressed as mice, and into an old storage closet that had been converted into a makeshift dressing room. Ellen, whose face was a pretty funky shade of green, sat slumped in an old barbershop chair. She stared glumly at her reflection in a gold-framed mirror mounted to the wall.

"She's sick," Stacy said.

Ellen spun her chair around. "I am not."

"Mr. Angelo said he thought Ellen would have to drop out of the play," Stacy continued.

"Don't be ridiculous. I'm not even that sick," Ellen said, "I just—"

Ellen broke off and clapped a hand over her mouth. "Excuse me." She stood up shakily and dashed out of the room.

"She's been puking all day," Stacy said.

"When did she get sick?" I asked.

"Beats me. But you know what this means, right? You'll have to take over. You're Cinderella now."

The thought of going onstage made me want to join Ellen in the bathroom and barf my guts out too. "No. No way, not going to happen. You guys will figure something out." I took two steps backward and bumped into Mr. Angelo, who held a box of props.

"Callie! Stacy! Just the girls I wanted to see. I heard

you were looking for this." Mr. Angelo pulled out a plastic wand and handed it to Stacy. "As you've no doubt heard, Callie, we've a situation on our hands." From the box he pulled out a plastic pair of glass slippers, and a plastic tiara.

While he talked, I took my glasses out of my pocket and put them on. If I was going to argue myself out of this, I wanted every advantage.

The air shimmered and the screen appeared by Mr. Angelo: *We'll have to adjust the costume for Callie, but I think it'll be okay. Good thing Ellen insisted on writing cue cards.*

"Yeah, I heard," I said. "And I'm telling you right now, I'm not doing it. Find another Cinderella, because I'm not going onstage, cue cards or not."

"Must I remind you that I once did something really nice for you?" Mr. Angelo said. "This is why we have understudies. You *will* go on as Cinderella tonight. And that's that." Mr. Angelo squashed the tiara on my tangle of curls and thrust the glass slippers into my hands. "Now start getting ready."

Ellen returned, her face now a very unnatural shade of gray.

"Ellen," Mr. Angelo said, placing an arm around her. "This is a terrible, terrible thing. To lose our Cinderella right before the curtain goes up. How horrible." Mr.

Angelo left, but not before I caught his last thoughts: *Oh thank heavens. That girl was going to ruin my play.*

"What is he talking about?" Ellen asked. Her eyes widened when she saw me wearing the tiara and holding the glass slippers. "He gave my part to *you*?"

She said it just like that. Like anyone in the world would've been a better choice than me. Like the entire play should be cancelled because she was sick. Which, I realized from reading the screen hovering next to her, was exactly what she thought.

"They can't cancel the play just because you're sick," I said.

"Yes, they can," Ellen said, not missing a beat. "And they will if they have no other choice."

"What do you mean?" I glanced at Stacy, who shrugged and shook her head.

"I mean, they'll cancel it if there's no one to play Cinderella. They'll have to reschedule the play for when I feel better. Cinderella's the lead, it's not like they can just give the part away at the last minute and expect someone to learn the lines—right?"

Ellen looked over at Stacy. "No offense." Then she turned back to me. "Tell Mr. Angelo you never memorized your lines."

Okay, that was actually a good excuse. I sort of wished I'd thought of it myself five minutes ago. But then I looked at Ellen, who crossed her arms over her chest, like she was just waiting for me to obey her, and I felt mad all over again.

"You want me to lie to Mr. Angelo?" I asked.

"I want you to help me."

"But memorizing those lines is half my grade."

"Since when have you ever cared about your grades? Or tell him something else. Tell him you're getting sick too. Please, Callie? Best friends forever, right?" Ellen held out her pinkie.

I looked over at Stacy, and the screen hovering beside her showed me she was picturing herself back in Oregon, with the braces and the dull hair. She sat alone in a classroom, while everyone around her clustered their desks together and worked in groups. The picture changed then, now Stacy was onstage, a spotlight causing her Fairy Godmother costume to sparkle and shine, while the audience below sat mesmerized. The picture changed again, and one thought scrolled across the blue screen: *No. Please, I want them to see me.*

"Please, Callie?" Ellen said, her pinkie still raised. "Do this for me?"

Ellen was asking me to do a horrible thing. But courtesy of my super freaky glasses, I could tell she was too caught up in her own thoughts to realize it: *I did not work this hard and have Tara fly down for the weekend so Callie could play Cinderella. I'm tired of hearing how great Tara is. She never had the lead in the school play. And I bet she would've stunk at playing the guitar if she tried.*

For as long as I could remember, Ellen seemed fearless to me. But watching her now and reading her thoughts, I realized she worried what other people thought about her just as much as I did.

And when I looked at Stacy, I saw that, in her thoughts at least, she wanted me to stand up to Ellen: *Please. I want them to see me.*

When I caught Stacy's eye, she opened her mouth to say something, then gulped and closed it quickly. Then she looked down, her cheeks turning red. No matter how much she wanted to be in the play, Stacy wouldn't tell Ellen what she really thought. She'd choose to stay silent and let Ellen get her way. I understood that. Wasn't I usually the same way?

But not this time.

"No." I couldn't believe the word actually came out of my mouth.

Ellen couldn't believe it either. "What did you say?" She lowered her arm.

"You heard me. I'm not doing it."

"Why not?"

I glanced at Stacy. "Because we've all worked too hard for one person to ruin everything, Ellen. Even if that person is you."

"Come on, Callie. Best friends help each other out," Ellen said. *And if you don't help me out, we are soooo not best friends. We won't even be friends.*

I stared at Ellen's thoughts and started to lose my nerve. I didn't want to be onstage, anyway. Wasn't that why I passed on being Cinderella in the first place? Was I ready to lose my best friend? But then again, hadn't I been losing Ellen all semester anyway? We didn't have much in common anymore—actually, I couldn't even remember the last time Ellen called me her best friend. And did I even want to be best friends with Ellen, if it always meant doing *what* she wanted, *when* she wanted?

I decided I didn't.

I hugged the glass slippers to my chest; they felt slippery in my sweaty hands. "Then I guess . . . we're not best friends anymore."

Ellen looked stunned. The screen hovering next to her went black and disappeared in a puff, like someone hit the kill switch. She turned and ran out of the room, muttering "traitor" as she passed me.

Stacy and I were both silent as Ellen's footsteps died away. With a sigh, I stuck the glass slippers on my feet. Then I toddled over to the barber chair and picked up Ellen's abandoned script.

"I'll just leave you alone to study," Stacy said.

"Okay." I looked up, and Stacy hurried out the door.

But not before I saw the smile on her face.

"Ten minutes till curtain!" Mr. Angelo yelled.

I tugged on my costume—a dress made mostly of rags— that hung too tight and too long since it was originally fitted for Ellen. I tucked a stray hair under the kerchief I wore and headed stage left to peek out the curtain.

"Word on the street is you're the new Cinderella," said a voice behind me.

I turned around and saw Charlie, dressed in his Prince costume. "So it seems," I said, bowing. "Will you be my Prince tonight?"

Charlie laughed, but then his face became serious. "Hey, are you going to the Sadie Hawkins dance tonight? I know it's short notice, but I was wondering . . ."

I lost track of what he said because the air shimmered and the screen appeared next to him. Inside, I saw an image of Charlie buying a box of Red Hots. The picture changed, and Charlie talked to a sulky-looking Raven while she held the door of our locker open and he slid a chunky red envelope inside.

Those Red Hots were for me, after all. They just hadn't come from Scott.

Did that mean Charlie liked me? Like, *liked* me, liked me? Could I like him back? Last year, Charlie Ferris was the nasty boy calling me Polka Dot. But this year, could he be someone else? I thought about how easy it was to talk to him, and how much he made me laugh. Charlie's dimple showed as he grinned at me. Why had I never noticed his cute smile?

"So, will you?" Charlie asked.

I snapped back to attention. "Will I what?"

"Go to the dance with me?"

"Oh—yes. Yes, definitely."

Charlie looked down, and rubbed an invisible spot on the floor with his shoe. "You know, I always thought Polka Dots were cute." He stopped talking then, but the screen hovering next to him showed me he had wanted to say more: *And I love your hair.*

Charlie liked my crazy-frizzy-dead-leaf-colored-hair? I wanted to tell him he needed to get his eyes checked. But then I had another thought. What if there was nothing wrong with Charlie's vision? Or my hair. What if *I* was the one who needed to change the way I saw myself? Maybe that was what Dr. Ingram had been trying to tell me all along. Maybe in so many ways, I really did need vision correction.

"You're up," Mr. Angelo said, coming to stand next to us.

"See you at the ball," Charlie said, scampering away before I could say anything.

"See you," I said weakly.

Mr. Angelo showed me where to stand, and I gulped as he slid in front of the curtain and began addressing the audience.

"Ladies and gentlemen, welcome to Pacificview Middle School's seventh grade presentation of . . . *Cinderella!*"

Applause poured from the crowd, and I peeked through the curtain, trying to make out faces in the audience. Mom sat in a nearly deserted row with three empty seats to her right, where Ellen's family should have been. With a pang, I realized the seat to her left was empty, too— where my father should have been. The screen appeared by Mom and I read her thoughts: *I could kill Nathan. I told him three times what time it started. Who cares if Callie wasn't actually going to be onstage?*

I felt my stomach drop. I was a few seconds away from stepping onstage. In front of a roomful of people. Was I insane?

Just pretend you're alone in your room acting out one of your stories, I told myself. *It'll be okay.*

"And I must tell you, ladies and gentlemen," Mr. Angelo continued, "we've had quite a bit of drama backstage as well. There have been some last minute casting changes. The role of Cinderella will now be played by Calliope Meadow Anderson . . ."

Mom paled and her thoughts changed: *Oh my poor girl. She must be so nervous. What's she going to do?*

The air shimmered frantically then and screens launched up by every single person in the audience. I shielded my eyes from the overpowering blue glare and felt dizzy from reading everyone's thoughts:

Man, does this guy ever stop talking?

I should have gone to the bathroom before we got seats.

How long is this thing anyway?

I'm hungry.

I'm thirsty. . . .

On and on it went, until my head hurt so much I had to take my glasses off. I panicked then, because if I couldn't wear my glasses onstage, I wouldn't be able to read the cue cards, which were written in Ellen's cramped handwriting.

"Ladies and gentlemen, I give you . . . *Cinderella!*" Mr. Angelo finished, and the curtain began to rise.

At that moment, I figured out my favorite part of Cinderella's tale. And I realized it wasn't the pumpkin carriage, the killer dress, the Prince, or even the ball—magical as that all was. No. My favorite part was when Cinderella chose to step out of the attic. When she walked down those stairs to the Prince's men below and showed everyone her true self. When she chose a future different from what she'd always believed was possible.

Quickly, I slipped my glasses into my pocket. And I remembered something Ana once said to me: *"I've seen you practice. I think you could do it."*

Ana was right, I thought as I crossed to center stage and spoke my first line.

I *could* do this.

Chapter 19

✻ ✻ ✻

Super Freaky Glasses Rule #18
With great sight comes great responsibility.

I'D LIKE TO SAY I WAS THE BEST CINDERELLA EVER. I'D like to say that when I spoke, my voice rang out strong and clear. I'd like to say all those things, but I'd be lying if I did.

The truth was I stumbled a lot. Literally—I kept forgetting to hike up Ellen's too-long costume when I walked across the stage. I forgot some of my lines. And when the Wicked Stepsisters made fun of me, I got nervous and spoke so softly I had to repeat the line. I wasn't too embarrassed though; it seemed like something Cinderella might have done, too. So being onstage wasn't totally horrible after all.

Actually, I sort of liked it.

When the curtain came down, I was surrounded by a swarm of ball gowns, oversize mice, Wicked Stepsisters, and an ecstatic Fairy Godmother, all congratulating me. I could still hear the applause as Charlie thrust a bouquet of roses into my arms, shyly telling me it was tradition. Everyone told me I'd been an incredible Cinderella.

Wondering what they *really* thought, I slipped over to the dressing room, where I had stashed my glasses during intermission. I had just put them on when I felt a tap on the shoulder. Behind me, Scott grinned.

"Nice flowers," he said, gesturing to the roses as I placed them on the dressing table. "You were awesome." The air shimmered and an image of Scott backstage, dozing on a couch, waking from the applause of a couple students next to him appeared on the hovering screen.

Okay, so he was lying. But everyone told little white lies like that. Over the past few months, I'd learned not to take it personally.

"I mean it," Scott said. "You're really talented. And I thought—with Ellen sick and all—maybe you would like to go to the Sadie Hawkins dance with me tonight?"

Scott was Ellen's boyfriend now. I shouldn't have wanted to say yes. But a part of me did, even though Charlie had already asked me. Another part of me felt evil for wanting to go to the dance with someone else's boy-friend. But if Ellen was sick, wasn't Scott supposed to stay home with her? Wasn't that the whole point of having a boyfriend?

And why did he ask me? Last time I checked, Scott thought I was a weirdo. His thoughts changed then, and I had my answer: *I am not missing that dance. Ellen will get over it. It's too bad Stacy already has a date. But at least Callie doesn't.*

Excuse me? Why did he think I didn't have a date? He never asked.

Instead of answering, I said what I'd wanted to tell him all semester. "I really liked the haiku you wrote."

"What?" Scott furrowed his brow. *Has she gone mental?*

"The haiku you wrote in English last year—I really liked them."

The screen hovering by Scott's head changed, showing a picture of him sitting at a desk—in what I assumed was his bedroom—as he copied something from a book. I squinted and read the title: *101 Romantic Haiku.*

"Yeah thanks," Scott said. "It's just something I like to do."

My mouth opened, but no sound came out. Scott Fowler was a liar. A. Big. Fat. Liar. And a bad boyfriend.

And just like that, my crush on him was gone.

"Well, how 'bout it? Want to go to the dance with me?"

I gave him the biggest smile I could and said, "Gee, Scott, I would've loved to. But I already have a date. No offense, but you're not my type. You're a little too— mental."

My dress swished noisily as I spun around and marched out of the dressing room and down the hall. As I rounded a corner, I smacked straight into Raven, who carried a stack of play programs. The programs fell from her hands and skittered to the floor.

"Watchit, loser!"

"Sorry, I'm sorry." I bent to the ground to pick up the programs and found a piece of blue paper that was crumpled and worn—like someone had been carrying it around for a while. When I smoothed it out, I realized it was the flyer I stuck in Raven's English textbook a few weeks ago.

"Here," I said quietly, standing up and handing it to her.

A screen sprang up next to Raven as she took it: *I knew it was from her. Maybe she's not a total loser after all.*

"Not totally, no," I said, and then flushed when I realized I'd spoken out loud.

Raven gave me a strange look and said. "Thanks. You

know, for . . ." She trailed off, and just waved the flyer slightly. Then Raven did something rare. She smiled.

But only briefly. Then her usual sneer slid back into place and she said, "This is a mess."

"Yeah," I said, quickly looking away from Raven and down at the scattered programs. "I guess we'd better pick them up."

"We?" Raven summoned her best Wicked Stepsister voice. "You're Cinderella. *You* pick them up."

Raven stomped off and I finished picking up the programs. Mr. Angelo appeared then, with several other students, including Charlie and Scott.

"Wonderful, excellent!" Mr. Angelo said. "I've never seen such a vulnerable interpretation of Cinderella!" The air shimmered, and a screen sprang up next to him: *She's saved drama's budget! This year, anyway.*

"Mr. Angelo!" Stacy came running up, cheeks flushed, and eyes sparkling. "That was waaay fun! Do you think I can wear my costume to the Sadie Hawkins dance tonight?" Everyone laughed while Stacy twirled around in her Fairy Godmother dress.

"I'm afraid not," Mr. Angelo said. "But I'll tell you what, you can keep your magic wand. How about that?"

Stacy grinned and held up the sparkly plastic wand.

With a swish of her hand, she waved the wand and pretended to turn Scott into a toad, and everyone laughed again (although Scott didn't seem to think it was that funny). Then Stacy held the wand out to me. "Actually, I'd like to give it to Ana. It should have been hers, anyway."

I took the wand. "Okay, maybe I'll stop by her house later, and see if her flu is any better."

Mr. Angelo nodded and said that was a good idea. But I barely heard him. Instead I stared at the words scrolling across the screen hovering next to him. *Flu? Well, I suppose it was easier for Ana to say that than to tell Callie the truth.*

I read those words and something in me went cold. A million tiny things clicked into place. The time Ana told me she was sick, and couldn't come to the Halloween carnival. How she wanted to join all those clubs, but then suddenly seemed to change her mind. How she never had clothes that fit well. The secret she wouldn't share with me that day in the park . . .

Even though I had a pair of magic glasses, had I been blind all this time?

Use your glasses wisely, Dr. Ingram's voice rang through my head.

And finally, I knew what that meant.

✸ ✸ ✸

Clutching the fairy godmother wand, I ran as fast as my glass-slippered feet would carry me, down the staircase and out the back entrance of the multipurpose room.

"Callie! Wait!" I heard Charlie call behind me, but I didn't turn around. I didn't even slow down—I wanted to talk to Ana *now*, before I lost my nerve.

A glass slipper caught on a crack in the sidewalk, and wrenched off my foot. I left it behind, and kicked off the other slipper as I ran out of Pacificview, down the street, and into my tract.

All was silent on Butterfly Way as I passed my house and hurried up the Garcias' front lawn. Through the window I saw the bluish glare of the television. Mr. Garcia's white SUV wasn't in the driveway. I bent over my knees, panting to catch my breath. Then I slipped on my glasses and rang the doorbell.

My reflection showed dimly in the glass door. My hair was snarled in the tiara, which hung lopsided on my head. Wrinkles and smudges of dirt covered my costume, and sequins were missing. I looked down, and saw my feet were dirty from running barefoot.

With a click, the door cracked open. Inside, I heard the beeping and zinging of a video game. Ana peered out

at me, her eyes were red and puffy, like she'd been crying.
When she saw my rumpled Cinderella gown her eyes widened. "Why are you wearing—"

"Can you come outside?" I said, cutting her off.
"Please?" I added, when Ana hesitated. "Just for a
minute?"

Ana ducked back into the house and said something to
Anthony and Miguel in Spanish. Then she stepped outside
and carefully closed the door behind her. She sat down on
the porch and hugged her knees to her chest.

I knelt down next to her and handed her the fairy godmother wand. "This is from Stacy. Are you okay?"

"I'm fine," Ana said, looking down at the wand.

Okay, I'd had the glasses long enough to know no one
meant it when they said they were fine. The air waved and
shimmered, and the screen launched up by Ana. As usual,
Spanish words—and some English words—scrolled across.
But I still couldn't understand much of it.

"Are you sick, Ana?" I asked. "Really?"

Ana didn't answer right away. But the words in the
screen hovering next to her changed. And for the first
time, I saw one full sentence in English: *Leave me alone.*

Normally, if I knew someone didn't want to hang out
with me, I *would* leave, faster than you can say coward. But

Ana wasn't sick. And I wasn't leaving until I found out why she lied to me.

"Come on. You can tell me. What's going on?"

Ana said nothing, and continued to stare at the wand, a sad look on her face.

"Please, Ana. Something's not right, and I want to know what it is."

Finally, the Spanish words vanished, and images flashed on the screen. Images of Ana and what I think her life must have been like these last few months: Ana showing Mr. Garcia a flyer advertising Pacificview's clubs, and Mr. Garcia shaking his head no. Ana, looking unhappy as she took the Garcia kids trick-or-treating on Halloween. Ana setting the table for dinner, and walking into the living room to call the Garcia family, who watched television. Ana standing at her locker, while a group of girls walked by, giggling and pointing to the long skirt she wore. Ana watching Mr. Garcia and Anthony and Miguel play video games in the living room. Mr. Garcia offered the controller to Ana, who politely shook her head no. Then she slipped away to her room upstairs, lay down on her bed, and began to cry.

Then one more image: Mr. Garcia yelling at Ana—shaking his head no at whatever she said in return. Then he picked up the phone and handed it to her.

"Did your uncle say you couldn't be in the play?" I guessed.

Ana closed her eyes and nodded. "He—what do Americans call it?—grounded me." She opened her eyes and took a deep breath. "I'm grounded because I lied to him. Yesterday I told him we were studying after school. But then your mom saw him out in the front yard this morning and she said something about picking us up from the pizza place."

"You *lied* to your uncle?" I asked, stunned.

"I just wanted to go out somewhere. Just once," Ana said in a high-pitched voice. "Tío has old ideas about girls. He thinks I should help around the house, and I must do well in school. But he doesn't approve of things like dances, or clubs, or girls our age going out without an adult." Ana began to cry, deep sobs that made her shoulders shake and her chest heave. I didn't know what to do or what to say, so I just put my arm around her.

I felt sick as I watched her cry. Because Ana had tutored me in Spanish, and listened to me talk about Ellen and Scott, and my dad. But had I ever asked her about *her* family? When had I asked her if it was easy moving to a new country and living with relatives she barely knew?

The answer was that I hadn't.

When Ana's sobs subsided I asked, "Have you told your parents any of this?"

Ana sniffed and shook her head. "My father is really sick. I don't want them to think I'm ungrateful. Tío sends them money, and he helps me with my homework. He bought me new clothes—even if they're a little . . ." She gestured to her long skirt and trailed off, like she was looking for the right word.

"*Feo?*" I supplied.

I saw the faint trace of a smile on Ana's face as she gave the English translation, "Ugly, yes." She paused, and added, "I don't think Tío understands very much about girls and middle school." Ana sniffed again. "Anyway, I haven't said anything to anyone."

"You could have told me," I said.

"I didn't want to tell *anyone*. I didn't want them to— how do you say it?—make fun of me? Some girls at school already make fun of my clothes." Ana began to cry again.

I thought back to the beginning of the year, and how nervous I was about wearing my glasses to school. I had been so certain everyone was just waiting to make fun of me. But most people hadn't. And the people who had— people like Raven—had their own worries.

One thing the glasses taught me: No matter how different we looked on the outside, on the inside we worried and wondered about the same things. We all hoped we'd find someone who would see us for the person we really were, and the person we wanted to be.

I opened my mouth to tell Ana all this, but right then she wiped her eyes and handed me back the fairy god-mother wand. "Keep this," she said, standing up. "I have to go. I have to make dinner for the boys before Tío gets home."

"Wait, Ana. Why don't you come to my house. Maybe—"

"I can't. And anyway, it's okay. I'm fine." Ana opened the front door, and said, "Good-bye, Callie."

The door clicked shut. And from the tone of her voice, I didn't think Ana meant, "Good-bye, we'll talk about this later." I thought she meant, "Good-bye. The next time you see me at school, please forget I ever said anything."

I stood up and walked across the lawn to my house, twirling the wand in my hand. My plastic tiara was still snaggled in my hair so I pulled it free. Under the spot-lights of the multipurpose room, the tiara and wand had glittered brilliantly. But now, with dusk settling, they both seemed dull and dim.

Right then I wished I really was Cinderella, with a real fairy godmother. Because I would tell my fairy godmother

I didn't need the beautiful dress, the magic pumpkin, or even the handsome Prince. I'd just ask her to wave her magic wand, and, in a puff of swirly smoke, give my friend the happy ending she deserved.

But then I had another thought. What if Cinderella never had to wait for a fairy godmother to show up? What if Cinderella had a friend? Would she have spent all those lonely years in her stepmother's house? Or would her friend have helped her find a different future?

My house stood silently before me, waiting, it felt like, for me to make a decision. I knew I could walk inside, pack away my Cinderella and fairy godmother gear, and pretend I believed Ana when she said she was fine. Or, I could choose to see that Ana really was miserable, and believe I had the power to help her.

I opened the door and walked upstairs to my room.

And I chose to see.

Chapter 20

✲ ✲ ✲

Super Freaky Glasses Rule #19

Sometimes using the glasses wisely means not using them at all.

"REMEMBER WHAT AUNT ROSA SAID. BE PATIENT, AND remember that these last few weeks have been hard for Ana," Mom said, pulling the car over to the side of the road.

I nodded and stared at Aunt Rosa's small house. Ana's new house, I reminded myself. Smoke swirled from the chimney and the windows glowed with buttery yellow light. White Christmas lights lined the rooftop, and through the window I saw a Christmas tree with blinking red and green lights.

I felt my glasses through my jacket pocket. I had them

ready to go if I needed them. Telling Mom about Ana and how unhappy she felt at Mr. Garcia's was the hardest thing I'd ever done. But when I finished, I handed her Aunt Rosa's phone number.

So Mom called Aunt Rosa, and they had a long conversation. The next day when I looked out my window, I saw Aunt Rosa leading Ana to a blue minivan. They drove away, and Ana hadn't been at school ever since.

Mom and Aunt Rosa had talked on the phone a few times since that day. Aunt Rosa told Mom she made it clear to Mr. Garcia she appreciated all the help he gave Ana—but it was *her* turn to get to know her niece.

"Apparently Esteban gave in pretty easily," Mom had said. "Rosa thinks he realized it wasn't working out. But," she added, "Rosa agreed it was wrong for Ana to lie—so she's still grounded. I'll take you to see her when she's off restriction."

Now I leaned my head back and listened to the rain tapping on the windshield. "What if she doesn't want to talk to me?"

"It'll be okay." Mom put an arm around my shoulders. Normally if she did that, I'd shrug her off. But this time I didn't.

"I don't know what to say to her."

"You'll think of something." Mom pointed to the notebook paper I clutched in my hand. "Give her the story you wrote. And tell her you miss her."

We got out of the car and walked up to the front porch. Mom rang the doorbell. As we waited, I folded up my story and stuffed it into my jacket pocket.

Aunt Rosa answered the door and beckoned us inside. I was reminded again of how much she resembled Ana. She even had Ana's smile—the kind that looked right at you.

Aunt Rosa swept me up in a hug and said, "Ana's lucky to have you for a friend."

I smiled back slightly. I wasn't so sure Ana felt the same.

Aunt Rosa led us inside, and as she and Mom chatted I looked around the house. It looked the same as I remembered from a few months ago. A fire roared in the living room, which was full of overstuffed chairs and overflowing bookcases. Silver picture frames lined the walls, most of them of five girls I figured were Aunt Rosa's daughters. The pictures showed the girls first as babies, then school-age, then a few graduation pictures.

"Mine are all grown now," Aunt Rosa said, following my gaze. "It's nice having a teenager in the house again."

Aunt Rosa pointed down a hallway and said, "Ana's room is first on the right. Why don't you go and say hi." Then she turned to Mom. "Would you like some coffee?"

"Yes, thank you."

As Mom and Aunt Rosa headed to the kitchen, I walked down the hallway. Ana's door was open and she sat cross-legged on her bed, reading a book. She wore a glittery red sweater and jeans that seemed to fit her well.

"Hey," I said. "Can I come in?"

Ana looked up and nodded slightly, but she didn't speak.

"I like your room." Near the closet was a white bookshelf busting at the seams with books and magazines—some had Spanish titles, some had English titles. A light green quilt with white and lavender butterflies covered her bed. Ana's backpack leaned up against a small desk in the corner of her room.

"I talked to Señora Geck yesterday," I said, sitting down next to Ana on her bed. "She said if I do okay on the final exam, I should get a B in her class . . . I don't usually get those," I added when Ana didn't say anything. "I'm taking Spanish again next semester . . . but if you don't want to tutor me anymore, I totally understand."

Ana frowned and said, "Are you saying you *don't* want me to tutor you?"

"No, that's not what I meant," I said quickly. "I just meant, you know, that if *you* didn't want to tutor me I would understand . . ." I trailed off. Ana and I sat there silently, staring at each other. I don't think either of us knew what to say. Then I asked her the question I'd been wondering for weeks.

"Are you mad at me?"

Ana looked down at her quilt and traced a pattern with her fingertip. "Aunt Rosa said as long as I keep my grades up, I can join whatever clubs I want at my new school." Ana looked up. "I'm not mad, Callie."

"So . . . does that mean you'll still be my tutor?"

Ana smiled. "*Le ayudaré.* I will help you."

"Okay." I put my hand in my pocket and grasped my glasses. There were a million other questions I wanted to ask Ana. About her family in Mexico, how long she wanted to stay in America, and I wanted to know what she really thought. But after a moment, I relaxed my grip, and zipped up the pocket. I figured with everything Ana had been through, she deserved her privacy.

"I have something for you," Ana said suddenly, standing up and walking over to her closet, where she pushed the door open. "Here it is." She pulled out a tall Christmas tin and handed it to me. "Open it."

Inside the tin, cinnamon and sugar popcorn was mixed in with Red Hots.

"Aunt Rosa and I made it," Ana said.

I clutched the tin and smiled. I knew this meant I wasn't just the girl Ana tutored. This meant I was Ana's friend, too.

"I have something for you, too," I said, pulling the notebook pages out of my jacket pocket. "I wrote you a story. If you want it, I mean."

"Like, totally, for sure," Ana said in her best California Valley Girl accent. "What is it about?"

"It's about a girl named Anarella."

"*Anarella?*" That was the first time I ever heard Ana sound sarcastic.

"Anarella, yeah. Anyway, Anarella lived with her family, and they were happy, but poor. One day, a prince came along and offered to let Anarella live with her in his castle. But it turned out, Anarella was really lonely there and didn't have anyone she could talk to.

"Then one day, Anarella's fairy godmother swooped in, not in a pumpkin carriage, but a blue minivan and took Anarella to another castle, one where she wouldn't be so lonely."

"And then what happened?" Ana asked softly. "What did Anarella do then?"

"I don't know." I handed Ana the story. "I was hoping we could finish it together."

Epilogue

Super Freaky Glasses Rule #20
Know when it's time to move on.

A FEW WEEKS AFTER SPRING SEMESTER STARTED, I received a call from Dr. Ingram letting me know my glasses had *finally* arrived.

"It's been a while," Dr. Ingram said when I slid into his examination chair. He grinned. "Seen anything unusual lately?"

"Not really." These days, I used my glasses solely for reading, and resisted the urge to stare at the screens and spy on people's thoughts. Well . . . except for that one time last week. I needed to make sure Charlie planned on asking me to the Valentine's dance. He did.

"Is school going well?" Dr. Ingram asked, holding up a pair of caramel-colored glasses and placing them on me. Funny, they didn't look nearly as dorky as I remembered. In fact, they looked sort of cute.

"Yeah, I joined a couple clubs, actually." I held still as Dr. Ingram flipped on the projector and tested my vision with the new glasses.

At Mr. Angelo's urging, I joined the drama club. I also joined a writer's club that met after school. I felt weird walking into the classroom the first time, but when I did, I saw someone I knew: Stacy. She waved when she saw me, so I sat next to her. Stacy told me that when she didn't have any friends in Oregon, she started keeping a journal— everything she wanted to say, but didn't have anyone she could say it to. She's actually really cool. I guess you could say we're becoming good friends. A bunch of us from the writer's club have started eating lunch together.

Ellen isn't mad at me anymore, but Stacy and I don't hang out with her all that much. Over winter break her mom finally bought her a guitar and agreed to pay for lessons. Ellen liked it so much she started a band with some other girls from school.

I still haven't seen my dad—he's asked me to come to Napa to visit him, and meet Brenda. But I told him I'm not ready for that yet.

Ana still helps me with Spanish, and sometimes I help her with her English assignments at her new school. Next weekend, Stacy and I are going to Aunt Rosa's to help them paint Ana's room. Ana wants me to design a mural for her wall like I have in my room. I've decided to paint a picture of a family of butterflies soaring over a meadow. I hope Ana likes it.

"Wonderful." Dr. Ingram flipped off the projector. "These seem to be a perfect fit. Or would you like to keep the loaner pair for a few more days?"

"Thanks, but no thanks," I said, handing him back the thick black frames. "I'm learning to see without them."